M000266134

The route to your roots

When they look back at their formative years, many Indians nostalgically recall the vital part Amar Chitra Katha picture books have played in their lives. It was **ACK – Amar Chitra Katha** – that first gave them a glimpse of their glorious heritage.

Since they were introduced in 1967, there are now **over 400 Amar Chitra Katha** titles to choose from. **Over 90 million copies** have been sold worldwide.

Now the Amar Chitra Katha titles are even more widely available in **1000+ bookstores all across India**. Log on to www.ack-media.com to locate a bookstore near you. If you do not have access to a bookstore, you can buy all the titles through our online store **www.amarchitrakatha.com**. We provide quick delivery anywhere in the world.

To make it easy for you to locate the titles of your choice from our treasure trove of titles, the books are now arranged in five categories.

Epics and Mythology
Best known stories from the Epics and the Puranas

Indian Classics
Enchanting tales from Indian literature

Fables and Humour
Evergreen folktales, legends and tales of wisdom and humour

Bravehearts
Stirring tales of brave men and women of India

Visionaries
Inspiring tales of thinkers, social reformers and nation builders

Contemporary Classics
The Best of Modern Indian literature

Amar Chitra Katha Pvt Ltd
© Amar Chitra Katha Pvt Ltd, 1984, Reprinted February 2014, ISBN 978-81-8482-035-5
Published & Printed by Amar Chitra Katha Pvt. Ltd., Krishna House, 3rd Floor,
Raghuvanshi Mill Compound, S.B.Marg, Lower Parel (W), Mumbai- 400 013. India
For Consumer Complaints Contact Tel : +91-22 40497436
Email: customerservice@ack-media.com

The route to your roots

BHEESHMA

Son of the beautiful goddess Ganga, the giver of life, the lad was born to greatness. Not only was he handsome and wise, he was also equally adept on the battlefield or in a regal court. As this tale reveals, Bheeshma is best remembered for his exceptional honesty and kindness. Who else would have uncomplainingly suffered the trials of kingship without its comforts? Who else would have chosen long years of loneliness just to pander to a father's whim?

Script
Kamala Chandrakant

Illustrations
L.D.Pednekar

Editor
Anant Pai

Cover illustration by: V.B.Khalap

Bheeshma

ONE DAY, KING SHANTANU OF HASTINAPURA, WHOSE FAVOURITE PASTIME WAS HUNTING, WAS WALKING ALONG THE BANKS OF THE RIVER GANGA IN SEARCH OF DEER AND BISON.

SUDDENLY A BEAUTIFUL MAIDEN APPEARED IN FRONT OF HIM.

SHANTANU FELL IN LOVE WITH THE MAIDEN, AT FIRST SIGHT.

O DIVINE MAIDEN! WHOEVER YOU MAY BE AND WHEREVER YOU MAY COME FROM, I WANT TO MARRY YOU.

O KING I SHALL WILLINGLY BECOME YOUR WIFE. BUT ON NO ACCOUNT MUST YOU ASK WHO I AM OR WHY I DO WHAT I DO..

AND YOU MUST NEVER SPEAK AN UNKIND WORD TO ME. THE MOMENT YOU DO EITHER, I SHALL LEAVE YOU FOREVER.

SO BE IT!

SHANTANU MARRIED THE MAIDEN AND THEY LIVED HAPPILY TOGETHER.

BUT HIS WIFE BEHAVED STRANGELY FOR A WOMAN. EACH TIME A CHILD WAS BORN TO HER, SHE DROWNED IT.

THIS IS FOR YOUR GOOD.

SHANTANU WAS TROUBLED.

IT SADDENS ME TO SEE EACH CHILD OF MINE KILLED. YET I DARE NOT QUESTION MY BELOVED WIFE LEST I LOSE HER ALTOGETHER.

HOWEVER WHEN THE EIGHTH CHILD WAS BORN —

STOP! WHO ARE YOU? O WICKED WOMAN, HOW CAN YOU MURDER YOUR OWN CHILDREN?

ALAS! YOU HAVE BROKEN YOUR PROMISE. I AM THE GODDESS GANGA. THIS CHILD SHALL BE CALLED GANGEYA AFTER ME.

I HAD TO KILL OUR FIRST SEVEN CHILDREN, TO REDEEM THEM FROM A CURSE. THE EIGHTH CHILD WAS TO HAVE BEEN MINE AND WE COULD HAVE LIVED TO- GETHER FOREVER.

BUT AS YOU HAVE BROKEN YOUR PROMISE, I WILL HAVE TO LEAVE YOU NOW.

I SHALL TAKE THE CHILD WITH ME.

AND GODDESS GANGA DISAPPEARED.

ALAS! I HAVE LOST BOTH A DIVINE WIFE AND A GLORIOUS SON, BECAUSE I WAS IMPATIENT AND WAVERED IN MY FAITH.

BUT SHANTANU DID NOT LET HIS PERSONAL SORROW AFFECT HIS DUTIES AS A KING. HE CONTINUED RULING WISELY AND WELL.

OUR KING IS TRULY THE WISEST AND NOBLEST OF MEN.

IT IS INDEED UNFORTUNATE THAT HE HAS NO HEIR.

AND SO THE YEARS PASSED.

THEN ONE DAY AS SHANTANU CAME ONCE AGAIN TO THE BANKS OF THE GANGES, HUNTING DEER —

GANGA SEEMS SUBDUED AND RESTRAINED. I WONDER WHY?

SHANTANU WAS AMAZED.

AN EXTRAORDINARY FEAT WHICH ONLY ONE WITH DIVINE POWERS CAN PERFORM!

THE BOY WAS GANGEYA, HIS SON, BUT KING SHANTANU DID NOT RECOGNISE HIM.

WHO COULD THIS GODLIKE YOUTH BE?

GANGEYA KNEW WHO SHANTANU WAS.

MY FATHER IS PERPLEXED. I WILL PLAY A TRICK ON HIM.

AND HE SUDDENLY VANISHED BEFORE SHANTANU'S VERY GAZE.

AT THAT MOMENT A THOUGHT SUDDENLY STRUCK SHANTANU.

COULD HE BE MY SON GANGEYA?

HE CALLED OUT IMPLORINGLY TO GANGA.

PLEASE SHOW YOURSELF AND THAT MARVELLOUS YOUTH. ISN'T HE MINE?

THIS IS GANGEYA, THE EIGHTH SON I BORE YOU.

HE IS UNSURPASSED IN WISDOM AND THE USE OF WEAPONS. HE HAS EARNED THE TITLE DEVAVRATA.

AND GANGA VANISHED.

SHANTANU TOOK DEVAVRATA AND RETURNED HOME JOYFULLY.

WHEN THEY REACHED HIS PALACE HE SUMMONED ALL HIS KINSMEN, THE PAURAVAS, TO HIM.

DEVAVRATA SHALL BE THE HEIR TO MY THRONE.

THE PAURAVAS LOOKING UPON THE GODLIKE YOUTH, ADMIRED HIM.

DEVAVRATA SOON EARNED THEIR LOVE ...

IN ALL BRANCHES OF KNOWLEDGE, BOTH WORLDLY AND SPIRITUAL, HIS SKILL IS UNSURPASSED.

... AND THEIR RESPECT TOO.

HIS STRENGTH AND ENERGY ARE EXTRAORDINARY.

SHANTANU WAS HAPPY TO HAVE SUCH A WORTHY SON AND HEIR. BUT STILL HE FELT LONELY AT TIMES.

AT SUCH MOMENTS, HE TOOK LONG WALKS, ALONE, ALONG THE BANKS OF THE YAMUNA.

ON ONE SUCH WALK —

AH! WHAT A DIVINE FRAGRANCE! WHERE IS IT FROM?

JUST THEN HE SAW A BEAUTIFUL GIRL APPROACHING.

WHO ARE YOU?

I AM SATYAVATI, THE DAUGHTER OF A FISHERMAN.

WHAT ARE YOU DOING HERE?

I FERRY PASSENGERS ACROSS THIS RIVER IN MY BOAT.

KING SHANTANU WAS OVERCOME BY A DESIRE TO MAKE SATYAVATI HIS OWN AND TAKE HER TO HIS PALACE.

HER FRAGRANT PERFUME SHALL FILL MY LONELY HOURS.

I SHALL GO AND ASK HER FATHER FOR HER HAND.

HE WENT TO SATYAVATI'S FATHER.

I WISH TO TAKE YOUR DAUGHTER FOR MY WIFE.

O KING! I CAN NEVER OBTAIN A HUSBAND FOR HER EQUAL TO YOU. BUT... I WISH...

WHAT IS IT THAT YOU WISH? NAME IT!

THAT THE SON BORN UNTO MY DAUGHTER SHALL REIGN AFTER YOU.

IF YOU CAN PROMISE ME THAT, SHE IS YOURS.

SHANTANU WAS DISMAYED.

HOW CAN I DISINHERIT MY DEVAVRATA?

HE RETURNED TO HIS PALACE, HIS THOUGHTS FULL OF SATYAVATI.

AND YET MY LIFE IS MEANINGLESS IF I CANNOT MARRY SATYAVATI.

AT HASTINAPUR HE PASSED HIS DAYS, LOST IN HIS LONGINGS. ONE DAY—

FATHER, WHY ARE YOU SAD? YOU HAVE EVERY-THING A KING CAN WANT— PROSPERITY, LOYAL SUBJECTS, AN HEIR...

SHANTANU WAS QUICK TO ANSWER.

YOU ARE MY ONLY SON. YOU ARE AN EXCELLENT ARCHER AND YOU WELCOME COMBATS.

SUPPOSING YOU ARE SLAIN, WHAT WILL HAPPEN TO THE BHARAT DYNASTY? IT IS THIS THOUGHT THAT WORRIES ME.

BUT DEVAVRATA WAS TOO INTELLIGENT TO BE TAKEN IN BY THESE WORDS.

I MUST FIND OUT WHAT SECRET LONGING NAGS MY FATHER.

SO HE WENT TO AN OLD MINISTER WHO WAS DEVOTED TO HIS FATHER.

REVERED SIR, WHY DOES MY FATHER GRIEVE SO?

HE HAS SET HIS HEART ON SATYAVATI, THE FISHERMAN'S DAUGHTER.

WELL. WHY DOESN'T HE MARRY HER? THAT SHOULD NOT BE VERY DIFFICULT.

THE MINISTER HESITATED FOR A SECOND. THEN—

HER FATHER WILL GIVE HIS CONSENT ONLY IF SHANTANU PROMISES THAT HER SON WILL BE HIS HEIR.

DEVAVRATA, ACCOMPANIED BY A FEW ELDERLY PAURAVA CHIEFS, WENT TO SATYAVATI'S FATHER.

WHAT IS YOUR OBJECTION TO GIVING YOUR DAUGHTER TO MY FATHER?

HE ALREADY HAS AN HEIR IN YOU. WHAT CHANCES WOULD MY GRANDSON HAVE AGAINST YOU?

HE WOULD BE CONDEMNED TO A LIFE OF SUBORDINATION.

UPON HEARING THESE WORDS DEVAVRATA TOOK AN OATH.

I VOW THAT THE SON BORN OF YOUR DAUGHTER SHALL REIGN AS THE KING.

BUT THE FISHERMAN WAS NOT SATISFIED.

I HAVE NO DOUBT THAT YOU WILL KEEP YOUR WORD. BUT WHAT ABOUT THE SONS YOU MAY HAVE?

DEVAVRATA DID NOT INTEND TO GO WITHOUT WINNING SATYAVATI FOR HIS FATHER.

CHIEF OF FISHERMEN, I HAVE GIVEN UP MY RIGHT TO THE THRONE. I NOW SETTLE THE MATTER OF MY CHILDREN.

AND DEVAVRATA TOOK A TERRIBLE OATH.

FROM THIS DAY I VOW TO REMAIN A BRAHMACHARIN*

BHEESHMA WENT TO SATYAVATI.

MOTHER, ASCEND THIS CHARIOT AND LET US GO HOME.

AT HASTINAPUR BHEESHMA TOLD SHANTANU EVERYTHING.

SON, FOR THIS I GRANT YOU A BOON. YOU WILL DIE ONLY WHEN YOU WISH TO.

SHANTANU MARRIED SATYAVATI AND HAD TWO SONS. THE ELDER WAS KILLED IN BATTLE. WHEN SHANTANU DIED, BHEESHMA SET THE YOUNGER SON, VICHITRAVIRYA ON THE THRONE AND RULED THE KINGDOM FOR HIM.

ONE DAY BHEESHMA APPROACHED SATYAVATI.

THE KING OF KASHI IS HOLDING A SWAYAMVARA FOR HIS THREE DAUGHTERS. VICHITRAVIRYA HAS COME OF AGE. I WOULD LIKE TO WIN THEM FOR HIM.

GO, BHEESHMA, WITH MY BLESSINGS AND MY GRATITUDE. WIN THEM FOR HIM.

BHEESHMA WENT IN A SINGLE CHARIOT TO KASHI AND WON THE PRINCESSES DEFEATING ALL THE RIVAL KINGS WHO OPPOSED HIM.

HE BROUGHT THE PRINCESSES AMBA, AMBIKA AND AMBALIKA TO SATYAVATI.

LUCK WAS WITH YOU, MY SON.

WHEN THE WEDDING WAS ABOUT TO TAKE PLACE, AMBA TURNED TO BHEESHMA.

IN MY HEART I HAD ALREADY CHOSEN ANOTHER. HE TOO HAD ACCEPTED ME. KNOWING THIS DO WHAT IS RIGHT.

BHEESHMA REFLECTED UPON WHAT SHOULD BE DONE, THEN DECIDED.

I GIVE YOU PERMISSION TO DO AS YOU CHOOSE.

VICHITRAVIRYA WAS MARRIED TO AMBIKA AND AMBALIKA.

AMBA WENT BACK TO HER CHOSEN LORD, BUT —

I NO LONGER WISH TO MARRY YOU AS YOU WERE CARRIED AWAY FOR ANOTHER.

AMBA WAS FURIOUS.

BHEESHMA IS THE CAUSE OF ALL MY SUFFERING. I WILL DESTROY HIM.

SHE WENT TO PARASHURAMA, THE SAGE WHO HATED KSHATRIYAS, AND TOLD HIM HER TALE.

I BESEECH YOU, O VENERABLE ONE. SLAY BHEESHMA AND AVENGE ME.

PARASHURAMA ACCOMPANIED BY AMBA AND OTHER ASCETICS WENT TO HASTINAPURA AND BHEESHMA CAME TO PAY HIM HIS RESPECTS.

WHAT CAN I DO FOR YOU, O VENERABLE SAGE?

YOU WILL MARRY AMBA.

I CANNOT BREAK MY VOW. BESIDES SHE WANTED TO BE FREE.

THEN I WILL HAVE TO SLAY YOU.

BHEESHMA AND PARASHURAMA MET EACH OTHER IN SINGLE-COMBAT AND FOUGHT FOR TWENTY-THREE DAYS.

AND BHEESHMA EMERGED THE VICTOR.

PARASHURAMA WENT TO AMBA.

I TRIED MY BEST BUT I FAILED. I ADVISE YOU TO FORGET YOUR HUMILIATION AND SEEK BHEESHMA'S PROTECTION.

I CANNOT.

AMBA PERFORMED SEVERE PENANCES FOR TWELVE YEARS TO WIN THE GRACE OF LORD SHIVA.

LORD SHIVA, AT LAST, APPEARED BEFORE HER.

WHAT BOON DO YOU SEEK OF ME?

I WISH TO SLAY BHEESHMA. HE HAS DEPRIVED ME OF MY RIGHTS AS A WOMAN.

YOU SHALL DO SO!

BUT I AM A MERE WOMAN. HOW SHALL I SLAY HIM WHO DEFEATED THE MIGHTY PARASHU- RAMA?

YOU WILL BE REBORN AS SHIKHANDIN, THE SON OF DRUPADA.

AND SHIVA DISAPPEARED.

AMBA MADE A FUNERAL PYRE, LIT IT AND JUMPED INTO ITS FLAMES.

I CANNOT WAIT TO DESTROY THIS BODY SO THAT I MIGHT ENTER THE NEW BODY THAT SHALL SLAY BHEESHMA.

AND AS SHIVA PROMISED SHE WAS REBORN AND BECAME SHIKHANDIN.

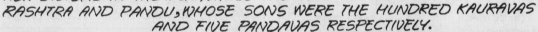

HER SISTERS IN THE MEANWHILE HAD HAD A SON EACH — DHRITA-RASHTRA AND PANDU, WHOSE SONS WERE THE HUNDRED KAURAVAS AND FIVE PANDAVAS RESPECTIVELY.

BHEESHMA SUPERVISED THE UPBRINGING OF THESE COUSINS AS HE HAD DONE THAT OF THEIR PARENTS.

BHEEMA ALWAYS BULLIES US!

AND THE ELDERS TAKE HIS SIDE!

THE CHILDHOOD ENMITY CONTINUED INTO THEIR ADULT LIFE.

IF THE PANDAVAS WANT THEIR SHARE OF THE KINGDOM, LET THEM FIGHT FOR IT.

GIVE THEM WHAT IS THEIRS AND AVOID TROUBLE.

BUT THE KAURAVAS DID NOT HEED HIM

AND WAR BROKE OUT BETWEEN THE KAURAVAS AND THE PANDAVAS — THE GREAT 18-DAY WAR OF THE MAHABHARATA. ON THE FIRST DAY OF THE BATTLE THE ELDEST PANDAVA CAME TO BHEESHMA.

VENERABLE GRANDSIRE, WE SEEK YOUR BLESSINGS AND YOUR PERMISSION TO BEGIN THE BATTLE.

BHEESHMA LOVED BOTH, THE PANDAVAS AND THE KAURAVAS, BUT HE WAS DUTY-BOUND TO FIGHT ON THE SIDE OF THE KAURAVAS. THEY WERE THE SONS OF THE REIGNING KING, DHRITARASHTRA.

FOR NINE DAYS BHEESHMA AND THE KAURAVA ARMIES FOUGHT RELENTLESSLY AGAINST THE PANDAVA ARMIES. DRUPADA'S SON SHIKHANDIN WAS AN ALLY OF THE PANDAVAS.

ON THE TENTH DAY OF THE BATTLE, ARJUNA, THE PANDAVA, SHIELDING HIMSELF BEHIND SHIKHANDIN, ATTACKED BHEESHMA.

SHIKHANDIN WAS ONCE A GIRL. I CANNOT ATTACK HIM.

HOW FORTUNATE THAT I HEARD THE STORY OF SHIKHANDIN LAST NIGHT.

THE TIME DRAWS NEAR. I WISH TO DIE BUT NOT AT THE HANDS OF SHIKHANDIN.

THEN HE FELT THE ARROWS THAT HAD PIERCED HIM DEEPEST.

THE FATAL ARROWS ARE ARJUNA'S! I AM READY.

AND BHEESHMA FELL.

BOTH ARMIES STOPPED FIGHTING AND CROWDED AROUND
THEIR BELOVED GRANDSIRE.

I NEED A SUPPORT FOR MY HEAD.

ARJUNA IMMEDIATELY PLACED THREE ARROWS UNDER BHEESHMA'S HEAD.

FINE! A PILLOW BEFITTING A WARRIOR. NOW I AM THIRSTY.

AT ONCE ARJUNA SHOT AN ARROW INTO THE EARTH NEAR BHEESHMA'S HEAD.

BHEESHMA DRANK AND WAS HAPPY.

THE BATTLE WAS RESUMED.

MY SOUL WILL DEPART ONLY AT THE AUSPICIOUS MOMENT I HAVE CHOSEN FOR IT. I WILL LIE HERE AND WAIT.

THE PANDAVAS WON THE WAR. YUDHISHTHIRA, THE ELDEST OF THEM, CAME TO BHEESHMA FOR HIS BLESSINGS AND HIS ADVICE ON THE DUTIES OF A KING. AS BHEESHMA FINISHED TALKING IT WAS THE AUSPICIOUS MOMENT HE HAD CHOSEN FOR HIS DEATH AND HIS SOUL PASSED AWAY.

DRONA

VALIANT ARCHER, SUPREME TEACHER

The route to your roots

DRONA

When Drona went to his childhood friend, Drupada, to remind him of his promise of eternal friendship made long ago, Drupada rebuked him and spurned him. Burning with anger and humiliation, Drona was filled with a desire for revenge. That was the only tragic flaw in a brave and supremely talented archer who taught the use of arms to the Kaurava and the Pandava princes.

Script
Kamala Chandrakant

Illustrations
P. B. Kavadi

Editor
Anant Pai

DRONA

DRONA, THE SON OF THE GREAT SAGE BHARADWAJA, WAS SO NAMED BECAUSE HE WAS BORN IN A 'DRONA' OR VESSEL.

BHARADWAJA HAD A FRIEND IN PRISHATA, THE KING OF PANCHALA.

DRONA IS A CLEVER BOY. LET HIM BE A COMPANION TO MY SON, DRUPADA.

AS YOU WISH, SIR.

THE TWO BOYS BEGAN THEIR STUDIES.

DRONA, A BRILLIANT PUPIL, SOON MASTERED THE VEDAS AND VEDANGAS.

DRONA, HOW I WISH I WERE CLEVER LIKE YOU.

BUT YOU ARE STRONGER.

ONE DAY BHARADWAJA CALLED DRONA TO HIM.

SON, NOW YOU MUST GO TO RISHI AGNIVESHA. LEARN THE SCIENCE OF ARMS FROM HIM.

ISN'T DRUPADA COMING?

I SHALL SPEAK TO PRISHATA.

BHARADWAJA APPROACHED PRISHATA.

THE GREAT RISHI FOR HIS GURU? CERTAINLY! DRUPADA IS FORTUNATE.

THE DAY OF THEIR DEPARTURE ARRIVED.

GO MY SONS, FINISH YOUR STUDIES. THEN MARRY AND FULFIL YOUR DUTIES IN LIFE.

DRONA AND DRUPADA LIVED FOR MANY YEARS IN THE ASHRAM OF AGNIVESHA. THEIR FRIENDSHIP GREW WITH THEM.

DRONA, LET ME WASH OUR CLOTHES. YOU RECITE SHLOKAS WHILE I DO IT.

YOU ARE KIND TO ME, DRUPADA. LISTEN THEN. ISHAVASYA-MIDAM...

YEARS PASSED. THEIR STUDIES OVER, THE YOUTHS GOT READY TO RETURN HOME.

DRONA, WHEN I BECOME KING AFTER MY FATHER, MY PALACE SHALL BE YOUR HOME. I PROMISE.

I SHALL ALWAYS REMEMBER YOU AND YOUR KIND OFFER.

A FEW YEARS LATER PRISHATA DIED AND DRUPADA BECAME THE KING OF PANCHALA.

THEN BHARADWAJA TOO DIED AND DRONA STAYED ON ALONE IN THE AUSTERE ASHRAM...

...BUT NOT FOR LONG.

MY FATHER WANTED ME TO MARRY AND HAVE SONS. SO SHALL IT BE.

DRONA MARRIED KRIPI, THE PIOUS AND INTELLIGENT SISTER OF KRIPA. WHEN A SON WAS BORN TO THEM A HEAVENLY VOICE PROCLAIMED—

THE CHILD SHALL BE CALLED ASWATTHAMA!

TO DRONA HIS GROWING CHILD WAS A CONTINUOUS SOURCE OF DELIGHT.

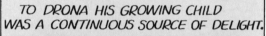

ASWATTHAMA EVEN SUCCEEDED IN DIVERTING HIM FROM HIS FAVOURITE PASTIME, THE PURSUIT OF THE SCIENCE OF ARMS.

THEN ONE DAY –

PARASHURAMA IS GIVING AWAY ALL THE WEALTH HE HAS ACQUIRED.

DRONA MADE HASTE TO THE ABODE OF PARASHURAMA.

O GREAT ONE, I HAVE COME FOR A SHARE OF THE WEALTH.

YOU ARE LATE. I HAVE NOTHING LEFT BUT THIS BODY OF MINE AND MY WEAPONS TO OFFER. QUICK! TELL ME! WHICH WILL YOU HAVE?

I CHOOSE YOUR WEAPONS WITH THE MANTRAS FOR THEIR USE.

THEY ARE YOURS.

PARASHURAMA GAVE DRONA WHAT HE WANTED, MAKING HIM SUPREME IN THE SKILL OF ARMS.

I HAVE THE BEST OF PARASHURAMA'S WEALTH. I CANNOT WAIT TO SHARE THE GOOD NEWS WITH KRIPI.

WHEN HE REACHED HOME —

KRIPI! ASWATTHAMA! I HAVE RETURNED!

ASWATTHAMA WAS PLAYING WITH HIS FRIENDS.

WHAT ARE YOU DRINKING?

MILK!

GIVE ME SOME.

THE BEGGAR'S SON WANTS MILK!

THEY MIXED SOME POWDERED RICE WITH WATER AND GAVE IT TO ASWATTHAMA, WHO DRANK IT AND WAS HAPPY.

I TOO HAVE TASTED MILK!

FIE UPON DRONA! HIS POOR SON DRINKS THAT STUFF AND THINKS IT IS MILK!

DRONA WAS MOVED AND ASHAMED BY WHAT HE SAW AND HEARD.

I SHALL TAKE KRIPI AND ASWATTHAMA TO DRUPADA. HE WILL WELCOME US AND HE CAN SHARE MY NEW WEALTH.

SO THEY SET OUT FOR DRUPADA'S KINGDOM.

IN DRUPADA'S PALACE ASWATTHAMA WILL DRINK THE RICHEST OF MILK, KRIPI. DRUPADA LOVES ME AS HIS OWN BROTHER.

DRUPADA, I HAVE COME. REMEMBER YOUR PROMISE TO ME, MY FRIEND? NOW YOU CAN FULFIL IT.

NO MEASLY BRAHMAN CAN BE A KING'S FRIEND!

AND WHAT IS THIS ABOUT A PROMISE? I RECALL NOTHING. BUT I CAN GIVE YOU FOOD AND SHELTER FOR A NIGHT IF THAT IS WHAT YOU SEEK.

DRONA WAS COLD WITH ANGER AND HUMILIATION.

I SHALL AVENGE THIS INSULT, DEAR DRUPADA, AND ALSO SHOW YOU WHAT FRIENDSHIP IS!

DO NOT GRIEVE, DEAR KRIPI. WE SHALL GO TO KRIPA. HE IS SURE TO WELCOME US.

KRIPA WAS THE GURU OF THE PANDAVA AND KAURAVA PRINCES AT THE KURU PALACE IN HASTINAPURA. HE WELCOMED THEM AS DRONA HAD EXPECTED.

DEAR KRIPA, FOR CERTAIN REASONS I WANT YOU TO KEEP MY PROWESS IN THE SCIENCE OF ARMS A SECRET.

LET IT BE SO!

ONE DAY THE KURU PRINCES CAME OUT OF THE CITY TO PLAY BALL IN THE OPEN COUNTRYSIDE.

OH! WHAT ILL LUCK! THE BALL HAS FALLEN IN.

I CAN SEE IT. BUT IT IS DEEP DOWN.

JUST THEN DRONA ARRIVED ON THE SCENE. NO ONE HAD SEEN HIM APPROACHING.

SHAME ON YOUR PRINCELY MIGHT AND YOUR SKILL IN ARMS!

THE PRINCES HURRIED TO BHEESHMA WITH THE NEWS.

IT IS NONE BUT DRONA. YOU ARE FORTUNATE. BECAUSE IN HIM YOU WILL HAVE A TEACHER BEYOND COMPARE.

BHEESHMA WENT IN PERSON TO MEET DRONA.

YOU HONOUR US BY YOUR VISIT. WON'T YOU COME TO THE PALACE?

AT THE PALACE —

BUT TELL ME, WHAT BRINGS YOU TO OUR CITY?

I SHALL TELL YOU ALL.

AND DRONA TOLD HIS STORY. THEN —

I COME SEEKING OBEDIENT PUPILS WHO WILL AVENGE MY INSULT.

YOU MAY CONSIDER IT AS ALREADY DONE.

BHEESHMA GAVE HIM A NEAT LITTLE HOUSE WHICH LACKED NOTHING.

YOU AND YOUR FAMILY SHALL ENJOY EVERY COMFORT THE KURU PALACE CAN GIVE YOU.

THEN HE BROUGHT HIS GRANDSONS TO DRONA.

O BRAHMANA, MAKE THE KURU PRINCES THE GREATEST IN THE SKILL OF ARMS.

AFTER DRONA HAD BLESSED THEM—

MY SONS, I HAVE A CERTAIN TASK FOR YOU. PROMISE ME THAT YOU WILL DO IT WHEN YOUR STUDIES ARE OVER.

ALL THE PRINCES REMAINED SILENT.

I PROMISE!

IT WAS ARJUNA, THE PANDAVA.

ARJUNA WAS AN EXCELLENT PUPIL AND SOON BECAME DRONA'S FAVOURITE.

THE GURU IS PARTIAL TO ARJUNA. HE DOES NOT LET ANY OF US SURPASS HIM.

ONE NIGHT, AS ARJUNA WAS DINING, A GUST OF WIND BLEW OUT THE LAMP. BUT ARJUNA CONTINUED EATING.

SUDDENLY AN IDEA STRUCK HIM.

I CAN EAT IN THE DARK OUT OF HABIT. I CAN MAKE SHOOTING IN THE DARK A SIMILAR HABIT!

ARJUNA BEGAN PRACTISING EACH NIGHT WHEN IT WAS PITCH DARK.

ONE DAY DRONA HEARD THE TWANG OF HIS BOW AND CAME TO MEET HIM.

I SHALL TRAIN YOU TILL NO BOWMAN IN THE WORLD IS A MATCH FOR YOU.

AND DRONA KEPT HIS WORD. NEWS OF ARJUNA'S SKILL SPREAD FAR AND WIDE AND PRINCES AND KINGS FROM NEIGHBOURING KINGDOMS FLOCKED TO DRONA TO BECOME HIS PUPILS.

I AM EKALAVYA, THE NISHADA PRINCE. I WANT TO BECOME YOUR PUPIL.

A MERE NISHADA! SUPPOSING ONE DAY HE EXCELS MY ROYAL PUPILS?

I AM SORRY. I CANNOT ACCEPT YOU AS MY PUPIL.

EKALAVYA, WITH BENT HEAD, SADLY RETURNED TO THE FOREST.

THERE HE MADE A CLAY IMAGE OF DRONA, WORSHIPPED IT AND...

...PRACTISED REGULARLY BEFORE IT.

ONE DAY THE KURU PRINCES CAME TO THAT FOREST TO HUNT.

ONE OF THEIR HOUNDS SAW EKALAVYA AND BEGAN TO BARK.

BEFORE IT COULD CLOSE ITS MOUTH, EKALAVYA SHOT SEVEN ARROWS IN SUCCESSION.

WHO ARE YOU? WHO IS YOUR GURU?

I AM EKALAVYA, A NISHADA PRINCE. DRONACHARYA IS MY GURU.

WHEN THEY RETURNED TO THE PALACE, THE PRINCES NARRATED THE WHOLE INCIDENT TO DRONA.

THE OTHERS LEFT. ARJUNA STAYED BEHIND.

HOW COULD YOU ALLOW A NISHADA TO EXCEL ME? YOU PROMISED...

COME, LET US GO AND SEE THE WONDROUS PERFORMER.

WHEN EKALAVYA SAW DRONA, HE FELL AT HIS FEET.

ARISE, MY BOY. IF YOU TAKE ME FOR YOUR GURU, GIVE ME MY FEE!

O ILLUSTRIOUS GURU, WHAT SHALL I GIVE? THERE IS NOTHING I WOULD NOT GIVE MY GURU.

I WANT THE THUMB OF YOUR RIGHT HAND!

WITH A SMILE ON HIS FACE, EKALAVYA CUT OFF HIS THUMB AND GAVE IT TO DRONA.

AND ARJUNA REMAINED UNEQUALLED.

AT LAST THE PRINCES HAD ALL BECOME SKILLED WARRIORS.

THE TIME HAS COME FOR ME TO EXACT MY FEE.

ONE DAY HE ASSEMBLED ALL OF THEM.

CAPTURE DRUPADA, THE PANCHALA KING, AND GIVE HIM TO ME. THAT IS THE FEE I WANT FROM YOU, MY ACCOMPLISHED PUPILS.

WE SHALL DO AS YOU SAY.

THEY MOUNTED THEIR CHARIOTS AND RODE OUT ACCOMPANIED BY DRONA.

WHEN THEY NEARED DRUPADA'S CITY—

LET THE KAURAVAS HAVE A CHANCE TO DISPLAY THEIR SKILLS. FOR THEY WILL NEVER BE ABLE TO CAPTURE THE MIGHTY DRUPADA. WE CAN EXERT OURSELVES AFTER THAT.

AS PLANNED, ARJUNA AND HIS BROTHERS WAITED AT SOME DISTANCE AWAY FROM THE TOWN.

DESTROYING THE PANCHALAS WHO CAME IN THEIR WAY, THE KAURAVA PRINCES LAID SIEGE TO THE CITY.

MEANWHILE DRUPADA HEARING THE UPROAR, CAME OUT OF HIS PALACE...

...AND BEGAN TO RAIN HIS ARROWS ON THEM.

THE KAURAVAS STUNNED BY THE DEFENCE, BROKE THEIR RANKS AND FLED, WAILING, TOWARDS THE PANDAVAS.

HEARING THE WAIL, THE PANDAVAS SALUTED DRONA AND MOUNTED THEIR CHARIOTS.

HE CUT DRUPADA'S BOWSTRING, COMPLETELY DISABLING HIM.

THEN SEIZING DRUPADA...

...ARJUNA LED HIM WITH HIS FRIENDS AND COUNSELLORS TO DRONA

WE HAVE BROUGHT YOU YOUR FEE.

THIS WAS THE MOMENT DRONA HAD PATIENTLY WAITED AND WORKED FOR.

YOUR KINGDOM NOW BELONGS TO ME.

DO YOU WISH TO REVIVE OUR FRIENDSHIP?

BRAVE KING, WE BRAHMANS ARE EVER FORGIVING.

I ASK FOR YOUR FRIENDSHIP AGAIN AND IN THE NAME OF FRIENDSHIP I WILL GIVE YOU HALF THE KINGDOM.

DRONA BEGAN TO LIVE IN HIS NEWLY-ACQUIRED KINGDOM BUT CONTINUED TO BE GURU TO THE KURU PRINCES.

YEARS PASSED BUT DRUPADA NEVER FORGAVE DRONA.

I SHALL HAVE TO SEEK THE HELP OF ONE WHO HAS EXCEPTIONAL SPIRITUAL POWERS TO ACHIEVE MY END.

SO HE WENT WITH HIS WIFE TO A VENERABLE SAGE.

WILL YOU CALL FORTH A SON FOR ME WHO WILL BE ABLE TO KILL DRONA?

GENEROUS KING, A SON SUCH AS YOU DESIRE SHALL BE YOURS.

HE PREPARED A SACRIFICIAL FIRE.

OUT OF ITS FLAMES ROSE A GOD-LIKE YOUTH.

THIS PRINCE HAS BEEN BORN TO DESTROY DRONA!

AND THEN, AMAZINGLY, THERE APPEARED A DAUGHTER TOO!

THIS GIRL WILL BE AN EXCEPTIONAL WOMAN AND WILL BRING ABOUT THE DESTRUCTION OF THE KAURAVAS!

THEN THE BRAHMANS GAVE THE BOY AND THE GIRL THEIR NAMES.

THIS GLORIOUS SON OF DRUPADA SHALL BE CALLED DHRISHTADYUMNA!

AND THIS DAUGHTER *KRISHNAA!

*LATER KNOWN AS DRAUPADI OR PANCHALI.

DRAUPADI BECAME THE WIFE OF THE PANDAVAS. THE KAURAVAS SUCCEEDED, BY UNFAIR MEANS, IN DEPRIVING THEIR COUSINS OF THEIR KINGDOM AND SENDING THEM INTO EXILE. AFTER THIRTEEN YEARS AND MANY ADVENTURES, THE PANDAVAS RETURNED TO ASK FOR THEIR KINGDOM. DURYODHANA, THE ELDEST KAURAVA, REFUSED TO PART WITH EVEN A SINGLE VILLAGE. WAR WAS DECLARED—THE GREAT 18-DAY WAR OF THE MAHABHARATA.
DRONA FOUGHT FOR THE KAURAVAS. DRUPADA AND DHRISHTADYUMNA NATURALLY BECAME THE ALLIES OF DRAUPADI'S HUSBANDS, THE PANDAVAS.

THEIR GRANDSIRE, BHEESHMA, LED THE KAURAVA ARMIES FOR THE FIRST TEN DAYS. ON THE TENTH DAY BHEESHMA FELL.

LET DRONACHARYA COMMAND OUR FORCES!

DRONA FILLED THE PANDAVA ARMIES WITH TERROR AND KILLED MANY OF THEM.

IN THIS MANNER HE FOUGHT FOR FOUR LONG DAYS.

ON THE FOURTEENTH DAY DRONA WAS ATTACKED BY DRUPADA.

BUT AFTER A FIERCE BATTLE, DRONA KILLED HIM.

DHRISHTADYUMNA WAS GRIEF-STRICKEN BY HIS FATHER'S DEATH. YUDHISHTHIRA CONSOLED HIM.

TAKE HEART, BRAVE ONE. YOUR FATHER'S DEATH SHALL BE AVENGED. YOU ARE BORN TO SLAY DRONA.

THEN KRISHNA SPOKE —

DRONA IS INVINCIBLE. WE WILL HAVE TO RESORT TO SUBTLE MEANS TO DEFEAT HIM.

TELL HIM THAT ASWATTHAMA IS DEAD...

NO! NO! THAT WOULD BE A LIE.

DRONACHARYA WILL BE DISABLED BY GRIEF.

IF THAT IS WHAT BOTHERS YOU, YUDHISHTHIRA, I SHALL KILL ASWATTHAMA THE ELEPHANT, AND...

THEN BHIMA WENT TO DRONA.

ASWATTHAMA HAS BEEN KILLED!

NO! IT CAN'T BE TRUE. I KNOW HOW SKILFUL MY SON IS.

DRONA REMEMBERED THAT YUDHISHTHIRA WOULD SPEAK ONLY THE TRUTH.

IS THIS TRUE, YUDHISHTHIRA?

YES. ASWATTHAMA THE ELEPHANT IS DEAD.

HE LAID DOWN HIS WEAPONS AND PREPARED HIMSELF FOR SAMADHI.

ASWATTHAMA! ASWATTHAMA! FOR YOUR SAKE I TOOK UP ARMS TO EARN A LIVING. NOW THAT YOU ARE DEAD I HAVE NO USE FOR THEM.

DHRISHTADYUMNA SEIZED THE OPPORTUNITY AND WITH ONE STROKE OF HIS SWORD SLEW HIM. BUT HE HAD ONLY KILLED A LIFELESS BODY. FOR UNKNOWN TO DHRISHTADYUMNA, DRONA'S SOUL WAS ALREADY ON ITS UPWARD JOURNEY WHEN HE STRUCK.

TALES OF ARJUNA

THE EXPLOITS OF AN EXCEPTIONAL WARRIOR

The route to your roots

TALES OF ARJUNA

Superbly skilled, speedy and strong, Arjuna boasted that he was the world's greatest warrior. But, despite his unquestionable courage, this honourable Pandava prince realised he could not confront Lord Indra's power – or even the wiles of a cheeky monkey – without help. He needed divine weapons, such as the Gandiva bow, with its inexhaustible supply of arrows, and a special war chariot. Most importantly, he needed the blessings of the gods, especially Lord Vishnu.

Script	Illustrations	Editor
Lopamudra	C.M. Vitankar	Anant Pai

ARJUNA, THE MONKEY AND THE BOY

ONCE, WHILE ARJUNA WAS ON A PILGRIMAGE TO VARIOUS HOLY PLACES, HE CAME TO RAMESWARAM.*

AND THAT IS THE BRIDGE RAMA BUILT WITH THE HELP OF THE MONKEYS.

MONKEYS? BUT WHY DID A GREAT ARCHER LIKE HIM NEED THE HELP OF MONKEYS?

HE COULD HAVE BUILT A BRIDGE OF ARROWS! WHY DIDN'T HE?

*IN COASTAL TAMIL NADU

THE BRAHMAN WENT HIS WAY BUT A MONKEY, WHICH WAS FOLLOWING ARJUNA, BURST OUT LAUGHING.

HA! HA! HO! HO! HA!

SURPRISED, ARJUNA TURNED ROUND—

A BRIDGE OF ARROWS WOULD HAVE COLLAPSED UNDER THE WEIGHT OF THE MONKEYS!

ARJUNA WAS A LITTLE ANNOYED BY THE MONKEY'S AUDACITY.

MERE MONKEYS COULD BREAK A BRIDGE OF MIGHTY RAMA'S ARROWS! IMPOSSIBLE! WHY, NO MONKEY COULD CRUSH A BRIDGE OF EVEN MY ARROWS!

I CHALLENGE THAT! A BRIDGE MADE WITH YOUR ARROWS WON'T WITHSTAND EVEN MY WEIGHT, PUNY AS I AM.

IF IT DOES, I AM WILLING TO BE YOUR SLAVE!

AND IF IT DOESN'T, I AM WILLING TO BURN MYSELF ON A PYRE!

SO ARJUNA SET TO WORK AND BEGAN TO BRIDGE THE WATERS BETWEEN LANKA AND THE MAINLAND WITH A SHOWER OF ARROWS.

WITH THE QUIVER OF INEXHAUSTIBLE ARROWS THAT LORD AGNI, THE GOD OF FIRE, GAVE ME, I SHOULD HAVE NO PROBLEM IN BUILDING A STRONG BRIDGE.

AS SOON AS THE BRIDGE WAS READY—

THERE! YOU CAN TEST IT.

THE MONKEY HAD BARELY TOUCHED THE BRIDGE...

...WHEN IT COLLAPSED!

NO! I CAN'T BELIEVE IT! I'LL TRY AGAIN.

THIS TIME ARJUNA SHOT THE ARROWS CLOSER, LEAVING NO GAPS BETWEEN THEM.

NOW TEST IT!

THIS IS STRONGER THAN I EXPECTED! I'LL WALK A BIT FURTHER.

BUT HE HAD HARDLY TAKEN A FEW MORE STEPS WHEN—

I HAVE LOST! I SHALL GET THE PYRE READY.

THE PYRE WAS MADE AND ARJUNA WAS ABOUT TO JUMP INTO THE FLAMES—

WAIT!

WHY DO YOU WANT TO GIVE UP YOUR LIFE?

ARJUNA AND THE MONKEY TOLD HIM ABOUT THE BET—

BUT A BET THAT HAD NO WITNESS IS NOT VALID.

I DON'T KNOW WHO YOU ARE AND WHY YOU WANT TO SAVE MY LIFE. BUT...

...I AM AFRAID YOUR WORDS ARE BORN MORE OUT OF KINDNESS THAN OUT OF LOVE FOR TRUTH.

HOW CAN YOU BE SURE THAT THE BRIDGE COLLAPSED BECAUSE OF THE MONKEY'S WEIGHT? THERE WAS NO ONE PRESENT TO JUDGE THAT!

WHY DON'T YOU TWO COMPETE AGAIN AND LET ME BE THE JUDGE?

THAT'S A BETTER SUGGESTION.

AS SOON AS THE BRIDGE WAS READY, THE MONKEY BEGAN WALKING ACROSS IT.

WHAT'S HAPPENING TO ME? MY STRENGTH IS LEAVING ME! I FEEL WEAK!

I'LL TAKE ON THE FORM I TOOK WHEN I LEAPT ACROSS THE OCEAN IN SEARCH OF SITA.

THE MONKEY MADE HIMSELF AS LARGE AS A MOUNTAIN...

...AND JUMPED UP AND DOWN ON THE BRIDGE.

WHAT! THE BRIDGE STILL STANDS! I CAN'T BELIEVE IT! ONLY KRISHNA.... WHY, OF COURSE THE BOY IS KRISHNA!

AT THE SAME MOMENT, THE MONKEY, TOO, REALISED THE TRUTH.

WHAT A VAIN FOOL I HAVE BEEN. OF COURSE IT IS THE LORD HIMSELF!

RAMA!

KRISHNA!

AND LO! IN THE PLACE OF THE BOY STOOD LORD VISHNU.

YES IT IS I! BOTH OF YOU NEEDED TO BE TAUGHT A LESSON IN HUMILITY. YOU, ARJUNA, WERE TOO VAIN.

AND YOU, HANUMAN, WERE TOO PROUD OF YOUR STRENGTH.

HANUMAN, TO FULFIL THE CONDITIONS OF YOUR WAGER YOU SHALL BE ON ARJUNA'S FLAG.

ARJUNA DEFEATS INDRA

A CERTAIN KING ONCE PERFORMED A SACRIFICE FOR TWELVE LONG YEARS, DURING WHICH OFFERINGS OF GHEE* WERE CONTINUOUSLY MADE TO AGNI.

WHEN AT LAST THE SACRIFICE WAS COMPLETED, AGNI WAS PERTURBED.

WHY DO I FEEL SO DULL AND WEAK? WHY AM I SO PALE? WHY DON'T I SHINE AS I DID BEFORE?

HE WENT TO THE ABODE OF BRAHMA.

O LORD, WHAT SHOULD I DO TO REGAIN MY LOST SPLENDOUR AND STRENGTH?

ALL THE GHEE YOU HAVE HAD FOR SO MANY YEARS HAS MADE YOU ILL.

* CLARIFIED BUTTER

9

BUT DON'T WORRY. CONSUME THE KHANDAVA FOREST, AND YOU WILL REGAIN YOUR LUSTRE.

AGNI HASTENED TO THE KHANDAVA FOREST AND BEGAN TO BLAZE, MUCH TO THE DISMAY OF INDRA.

IF I DON'T STOP THIS, MY FRIEND, TAKSHAKA, KING OF THE NAGAS, AND HIS FOLLOWERS WILL PERISH IN THE BURNING FOREST!

SO INDRA SENT DOWN HEAVY SHOWERS.

AGNI WENT BACK TO BRAHMA.

LORD, INDRA IS BENT ON THWARTING ME! WHAT SHOULD I DO?

THERE ARE ONLY TWO PERSONS WHO CAN HELP YOU: THE VALIANT HEROES, ARJUNA AND KRISHNA. GO TO THEM. THEY ARE NOW NEAR THE KHANDAVA FOREST.

AT THAT MOMENT, ARJUNA AND KRISHNA WERE RELAXING ON THE BANK OF THE YAMUNA.

THIS HAS BEEN AN UN-USUALLY HOT SUMMER. I FEEL AS IF I AM BEING SCORCHED BY AGNI!

AGNI WAS INDEED NEAR BY, IN THE GUISE OF A BRAHMAN.

AH! THOSE TWO MUST BE ARJUNA AND KRISHNA, THE FOREMOST AMONG MEN AND WARRIORS.

I AM A HUNGRY BRAHMAN. GRATIFY ME BY GIVING ME A LOT OF FOOD.

TELL US WHAT YOU WISH TO EAT, HOLY ONE, AND WE SHALL TRY TO GIVE IT TO YOU.

AGNI TOLD THEM WHO HE WAS AND WHY HE HAD COME TO THEM —

WE CAN TACKLE MANY INDRAS. BUT WE DO NOT HAVE THE WEAPONS TO MATCH OUR SKILL AND SPEED. WE ALSO NEED A GOOD CHARIOT.

THEN I SHALL GIVE YOU ALL THESE.

AGNI CLOSED HIS EYES AND THOUGHT OF VARUNA.

O VARUNA, BRING THE GANDIVA BOW, WITH ITS INEXHAUSTIBLE QUIVERS, FOR ARJUNA. BRING FOR HIM ALSO A CHARIOT; AND FOR KRISHNA, THE SUDARSHANA DISCUS.

IN A FLASH, VARUNA PLACED ALL THE WEAPONS AND THE CHARIOT BEFORE HIM.

ALL THIS IS YOURS.

O AGNI! WITH THESE WEAPONS NO ONE CAN WITHSTAND US. NOW EAT AS MUCH AS YOU LIKE! SURROUND THE FOREST WITH FIRE.

URGED ON BY THEM, AGNI CHANGED HIS FORM. HE THEN BROKE OUT INTO SEVEN FLAMES AND SURROUNDED THE FOREST, SETTING IT ABLAZE ON ALL SIDES. AS THE FLAMES ROSE HIGH, KRISHNA TURNED TO ARJUNA.

I'LL TAKE ON THE DENIZENS OF THE FOREST AND YOU TAKE ON INDRA AND THE CELESTIALS.

AS THEY POSTED THEMSELVES ON OPPOSITE SIDES OF THE FOREST, THE SKIES SUDDENLY DARKENED.

THUNDERCLOUDS! INDRA HAS STRUCK AGAIN!

THE NEXT MOMENT THE RAIN CAME DOWN IN TORRENTS.

THE FOREST, CHOKED WITH SMOKE AND STRUCK BY LIGHTNING, WAS FEARFUL TO LOOK AT.

I MUST BE QUICK! AT THIS RATE AGNI WILL BE SMOTHERED.

ARJUNA STOPPED THE SHOWER WITH A SHOWER OF HIS OWN...

... TILL THE FOREST WAS COVERED WITH A CANOPY OF ARROWS.

THERE! NOT A DROP OF RAIN SHALL TOUCH AGNI. NOT A SINGLE CREATURE SHALL ESCAPE!

BUT, THE NEXT MOMENT, INDRA RAISED A VIOLENT GALE...

... THAT HIT ARJUNA.

WHEN ARJUNA REGAINED CONSCIOUSNESS HE WAS FURIOUS.

I WILL NOT REST TILL I'VE VANQUISHED YOU, O KING OF THE DEVAS!

AND HE BEGAN TO AIM HIS ARROWS AT INDRA IN THE SKIES.

INDRA RETORTED WITH THUNDER AND FLASHES OF LIGHTNING.

SUDDENLY ALL WAS QUIET —

THE ENERGY HAS GONE OUT OF MY THUNDER!

THE WIND HAS BLOWN AWAY ALL THE CLOUDS. ARJUNA HAS USED THE VAYAVYA WEAPON AGAINST ME!

THE NEXT MOMENT THE SKY WAS CLEAR. THE SUN SHONE BRIGHTLY AND A COOL BREEZE FANNED AGNI AS HE BLAZED AFRESH. SUDDENLY —

KRISHNA! LOOK! IT'S INDRA AND THE DEVAS!

AND LOOK! ON THE OTHER SIDE THE ASURAS AND NAGAS ARE CHARGING FORWARD!

ARJUNA, YOU TAKE ON THE DEVAS...

...AND I'LL DEAL WITH THE ASURAS AND NAGAS.

KRISHNA SENT HIS DISCUS FLYING THROUGH THE AIR, AND THE NAGAS AND ASURAS FLED IN TERROR. MEANWHILE, ARJUNA COUNTERED THE ATTACK OF THE DEVAS SO SKILFULLY...

... *THAT THEY RETREATED IN PANIC. INDRA COULD NOT HELP ADMIRING ARJUNA.*

MY DEVAS ARE TURNING AWAY IN FEAR! ARJUNA HAS SURPASSED HIMSELF.

BUT, ALL THE SAME, HE SENT DOWN A SHOWER OF STONES.

LET ME SEE THE EXTENT OF YOUR MIGHT.

BUT ARJUNA QUICKLY WARDED OFF THE SHOWER WITH HIS ARROWS.

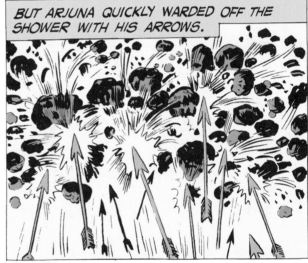

INDRA THEN TORE UP THE PEAK OF THE MANDARA MOUNTAIN ...

...AND HURLED IT AT ARJUNA.

BUT ARJUNA SMASHED IT WITH HIS ARROWS.

I AM PLEASED! HIS VALOUR IS UNMATCHED! AND KRISHNA HAS VANQUISHED THE ASURAS AND NAGAS WITH HIS DISCUS! IF IT WERE NOT FOR TAKSHAKA I WOULD----

AT THAT MOMENT A VOICE ECHOED FROM THE HEAVENS.

YOUR FRIEND, TAKSHAKA, IS SAFE. WHEN THE FIRE BROKE OUT, HE WAS AT KURUKSHETRA, O INDRA! NO ONE CAN DEFEAT ARJUNA AND KRISHNA. AND THE DESTRUC- TION OF KHANDAVA HAS BEEN ORDAINED BY FATE. SO GIVE UP THE FIGHT.

AS THEY SAW INDRA RETREATING, ARJUNA AND KRISHNA LEAPT FOR JOY.

SUDDENLY—

LOOK, IT'S THE ASURA, MAYA! HE WAS HIDING IN THAT CAVE! I'LL GET HIM WITH MY DISCUS.

BUT HE HAD BARELY RAISED HIS DISCUS...

... WHEN THE ASURA FLED TO ARJUNA.

O ARJUNA, PROTECT ME!

SINCE YOU ASK FOR MY PROTECTION, YOU SHALL HAVE IT.

ARJUNA HAS GIVEN HIS WORD. LEAVE HIM ALONE, AGNI.

WHEN QUIET WAS RESTORED, AGNI BLAZED FORTH FOR FIFTEEN DAYS TILL HE REGAINED HIS LOST LUSTRE.

INDRA THEN CAME DOWN—

FOR YOUR VALOUR AND MIGHT, YOU DESERVE A BOON EACH. ASK FOR ONE THAT IS NOT AVAILABLE TO MEN.

BESTOW ALL THE WEAPONS ON ME WITH THE KNOWLEDGE OF HOW TO USE THEM.

MAY MY FRIENDSHIP WITH ARJUNA LAST FOR EVER.

SO BE IT, KRISHNA. AND YOU ARJUNA, SHALL RECEIVE THE WEAPONS WHEN YOU NEED THEM MOST.

AS INDRA WENT AWAY, IT WAS AGNI'S TURN TO BESTOW A REWARD—

I HAVE BEEN GRATIFIED BY YOU. YOU SHALL, AT MY COMMAND, BE ABLE TO TRAVEL ANYWHERE AT WILL.

WHEN AGNI LEFT, ARJUNA, KRISHNA AND MAYA RELAXED ON THE BANK OF A RIVER.

O ARJUNA, YOU PROTECTED ME FROM THE WRATH OF KRISHNA AND AGNI. TELL ME WHAT I CAN DO FOR YOU.

BE EVER WELL-DISPOSED TO US, MAYA, AS WE ARE TO YOU.

BUT I MUST DO SOMETHING FOR YOU.

WELL, KRISHNA, WHAT CAN WE ASK OF OUR FRIEND?

MAYA, YOU ARE THE GREAT ARCHITECT OF THE ASURAS. WHY DON'T YOU BUILD A SABHA* FOR YUDHISHTHIRA? BUILD ONE THAT WILL BE UNSURPASSED IN SPLENDOUR.

* HALL

AND THAT WAS HOW YUDHISHTHIRA ACQUIRED THE MAGNIFICENT HALL THAT BECAME THE LAST STRAW FOR HIS ALREADY ENVIOUS COUSINS, THE KAURAVAS, AND INDUCED THEM TO DECEITFULLY DEPRIVE YUDHISHTHIRA OF HIS KINGDOM.

ARJUNA HUMBLED

AH! KRISHNA, NOW THAT THE GANDIVA BOW IS MINE, NO ONE CAN DEFEAT ME. EVEN INDRA WAS HELPLESS AGAINST MY ARROWS!

ARJUNA, THE PANDAVA, HAD COME TO VISIT KRISHNA AT DWARKA.

SUDDENLY, THEY HEARD A LOUD CRY.

WHAT'S THAT SOUND?

SEEING A BRAHMAN OUTSIDE, THEY WENT TO HIM —

WHAT IS TROUBLING YOU, FRIEND?

EIGHT TIMES HAVE I APPEALED TO OUR KING TO SAVE MY DEAD SONS AND EIGHT TIMES HAS HE IGNORED ME! NOW I HAVE LOST MY NINTH SON!

THOUGH HE IS A WARRIOR, HE IS FOND OF PLEASURE. IF HE HAD CONTROL OVER HIMSELF, WOULD HE BE SO CALLOUS?

A KING SHOULD PROTECT HIS SUBJECTS FROM EVERY CALAMITY INCLUDING DEATH. RESTORE MY SON TO ME, I IMPLORE YOU!

WHY DOESN'T KRISHNA RESPOND? HAS HE LOST ALL COMPASSION?

WHEN THE BRAHMAN CONTINUED TO LAMENT, ARJUNA COULD NO LONGER BEAR IT.

DON'T GRIEVE, MY FRIEND. I WILL PROTECT THE NEXT SON BORN TO YOU. IF I FAIL, I WILL BURN MYSELF ON A PYRE FOR MAKING A FALSE PROMISE.

THE BRAHMAN LOOKED SCEPTICALLY AT HIM.

WHEN BALARAMA, PRADYUMNA AND ANIRUDDHA — ALL MIGHTY WARRIORS — COULD NOT PROTECT MY SONS, HOW CAN YOU?

ARJUNA'S VANITY WAS STUNG.

I MAY NOT BE YOUR BALARAMA OR KRISHNA — BUT I AM ARJUNA, THE PANDAVA, AND I WIELD THE GANDIVA BOW.

I WILL SAVE YOUR SON FOR YOU. I WILL DEFEAT EVEN YAMA, THE GOD OF DEATH, IF NECESSARY.

NOW GO HOME AND LET ME KNOW WHEN YOUR WIFE IS ABOUT TO DELIVER HER TENTH CHILD. I WILL WAIT IN DWARKA TILL THEN.

SOME TIME LATER —

ARJUNA! COME! IT IS TIME! PLEASE SAVE MY SON FROM THE CLUTCHES OF DEATH.

ARJUNA SNATCHED THE GANDIVA BOW...

... AND WENT WITH THE BRAHMAN.

THERE! MY WIFE IS LYING IN THAT HUT.

ARJUNA RAISED HIS BOW...

...AND COVERED THE HUT WITH A THICK NETWORK OF ARROWS.

THEN HE STOOD GUARD OUTSIDE.

NOW LET US SEE IF THE LORD OF DEATH CAN DARE ENTER THE HUT.

SUDDENLY—

WAH-AH-AH!

AH! A BABY'S CRY! MY TENTH SON HAS SURVIVED!

WHERE'S THE BABY? WHY ARE YOU WEEPING?

HE...HE...CRIED A LITTLE AFTER HE WAS BORN...AND...THEN... JUST VANISHED!

THE BRAHMAN RUSHED OUT OF THE HUT LIKE ONE POSSESSED.

WHERE IS MY SON? BEFORE I HAD AT LEAST, BEHELD MY DEAD CHILDREN. THIS TIME I DIDN'T EVEN SEE MY CHILD!

YOU HAD PROMISED TO SAVE MY CHILD! YOU HAVE BROKEN YOUR PROMISE!

BE PATIENT, FRIEND. I'LL BRING YOUR SON BACK TO YOU.

MOUNTING HIS CHARIOT, ARJUNA SEARCHED HIGH...

... AND LOW. BUT NOWHERE COULD HE FIND THE BRAHMAN'S SON.

I'D BETTER RETURN AND GIVE UP MY LIFE. I HAVE FAILED.

I CAN SEE YOU HAVE FAILED. WHY HAVE YOU COME BACK?

TO FULFIL THE SECOND HALF OF MY PROMISE.

ARJUNA SOON HAD A PYRE PREPARED.

AS HE WAS ABOUT TO JUMP INTO IT—

WAIT, ARJUNA!

DO NOT PUNISH YOURSELF. I WILL SHOW YOU WHERE THE BRAHMAN'S SONS ARE. COME WITH ME.

THE BEMUSED ARJUNA GOT INTO THE CHARIOT—

WE WILL GO TOWARDS THE WEST.

THEY DROVE ON TILL THEY CAME TO THE REGIONS OF THE NIGHT.

OH! I CAN'T SEE A THING! ARE YOU THERE KRISHNA? HAS THE CHARIOT STOPPED?

THE HORSES HAVE STOPPED BECAUSE OF THE BLINDING DARKNESS.

KRISHNA RAISED HIS DISCUS—

GO, SUDARSHANA! LIGHT OUR PATH.

KRISHNA'S DISCUS WHIRRED ON AHEAD CUTTING WITH ITS OWN LUSTRE A BRIGHT PATH THROUGH THE DARKNESS.

SOON THEY REACHED THE OCEAN OF MILK, THE ABODE OF VISHNU. KRISHNA BOWED TO THE LORD, OF WHOM HE WAS BUT A PART.

ARJUNA STOOD DAZED FOR A MOMENT. THEN HE, TOO, BOWED IN REVERENCE.

I HAD THESE BRAHMAN BOYS BROUGHT HERE ONLY TO GIVE YOU AN OPPORTUNITY TO COME HERE. SLAY THE ASURAS AND HELP PRESERVE THE DIVINE LAW. THAT IS YOUR MISSION. AFTER FINISHING IT, COME BACK QUICKLY TO ME.

AH! KRISHNA, YOU KNEW ALL ALONG THAT THEY WERE HERE! NO WONDER YOU WERE SILENT AND UNMOVED.

AND THEN ARJUNA REALISED WHY THIS WHOLE DRAMA HAD BEEN PLAYED.

O KRISHNA, I NOW UNDERSTAND. WHATEVER MANLINESS AND POWERS A MAN MAY HAVE, IT IS ALL THROUGH THE GRACE OF GOD. FORGIVE ME MY VANITY.

TAKING THEIR LEAVE OF VISHNU, KRISHNA AND ARJUNA PUT THE TEN SONS OF THE BRAHMAN IN THE CHARIOT AND LEFT FOR DWARAKA.

IT IS FAITH IN GOD AND HUMILITY THAT ULTIMATELY WINS OUR BATTLES FOR US, ARJUNA, NOT VANITY OR SKILL ALONE.

AMAR CHITRA KATHA

5-IN-1

Five theme-based titles in every collection

5-IN-1
STORIES OF RAMA

5-IN-1
STORIES OF SHIVA

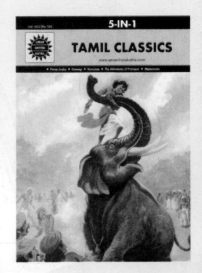

5-IN-1
TAMIL CLASSICS

Hard-bound editions that every generation will cherish

5-IN-1
BRAVE WOMEN OF INDIA

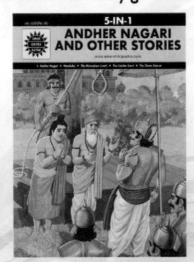

5-IN-1
ANDHER NAGARI AND OTHER STORIES

5-IN-1
THE GREAT MUGHALS

Over 40 titles available

All titles available on www.amarchitrakatha.com.

KARNA

BRAVE, GENEROUS, ILL-FATED PRINCE

The route to your roots

KARNA

Karna is one of the most poignant characters of the Mahabharata - generous to a fault but with shades of grey. Although born to princess Kunti and the sun god Surya, he grew up as the son of a humble charioteer. His talent and ambition, however, would not allow him to languish in anonymity. The Kaurava prince, Duryodhana, recognised his ability at archery and made him king of Anga. For this, Karna remained loyal to him till the end. He met an untimely end at the hands of his brother Arjuna in the Mahabharata War.

Script
Kamala Chandrakant

Illustrations
Ram Waeerkar

Editor
Anant Pai

Cover illustration by: Ramesh Umrotkar

Karna

RAJA KUNTIBHOJA, OF THE ILLUSTRIOUS YADAVA RACE, HAD NO CHILDREN. SO HE ADOPTED PRITHA, HIS NIECE, AND CALLED HER KUNTI.

1

ONE DAY SAGE DURVASA, FEARED FOR HIS VIOLENT TEMPER AND HARD TO PLEASE, VISITED RAJA KUNTIBHOJA.

THE VENERABLE SAGE WILL BE OUR GUEST. LOOK AFTER HIM WELL.

FOR A FULL YEAR KUNTI LOOKED AFTER THE SAGE CAREFULLY, PATIENTLY AND WITH DEVOTION.

I AM GLAD THE YEAR IS ALMOST COME TO AN END WITHOUT A MISHAP.

AND DURVASA WAS WELL PLEASED.

I WILL GIVE YOU A DIVINE MANTRA*. IT WILL ENABLE YOU TO CALL UPON ANY GOD TO COME AND BLESS YOU WITH A SON WHO IS IN EVERY WAY HIS EQUAL.

* A WORD OR WORDS OF POWER.

2

AS SOON AS DURVASA LEFT —

I WONDER IF IT REALLY WORKS. OH! LORD SURYA SMILES AT ME. I WILL CALL HIM DOWN.

THE MANTRA OF COURSE WORKED.

YOU SHALL HAVE THE SON YOU DESIRE.

BUT I AM NOT MARRIED. I WAS ONLY CURIOUS TO SEE IF YOU WOULD COME. PLEASE, PLEASE GO BACK.

BUT SURYA COULD NOT GO, AS THE SPELL OF THE MANTRA HELD HIM. AND KARNA WAS BORN, WITH THE ①KAVACHA AND THE ②KUNDALAS — A GIFT FROM HIS DIVINE FATHER ③SURYA.

① ARMOUR
② EAR-RINGS
③ THE SUN-GOD

3

AH! DEAR SON, FORGIVE ME. IF I EVER SEE YOU AGAIN, WILL I HAVE THE STRENGTH TO ACKNOWLEDGE YOU THEN?

FURTHER DOWN THE RIVER A CHILDLESS CHARIOTEER ADHIRATHA SAW THE BASKET AND LOOKED INTO IT.

AH! WHAT A BEAUTIFUL CHILD, ABANDONED BY SOME HEART-LESS MOTHER, NO DOUBT.

HE TOOK THE CHILD HOME TO HIS WIFE, RADHA.

LET US CALL HIM VASUSHENA OF THE KAVACHA AND KUNDALAS.

HE SHALL BE RADHEYA, DEAR WIFE - RADHEYA THE SON OF RADHA.

KARNA'S EARLY CHILDHOOD WAS A HAPPY ONE.

KUNTI MEANWHILE HAD MARRIED KING PANDU OF HASTINAPURA, WHO RULED THE KINGDOM FOR HIS BLIND BROTHER DHRITARASHTRA.

BUT KING PANDU BECAUSE OF A CURSE COULD NOT HAVE CHILDREN. SO HE RETIRED WITH HIS TWO QUEENS, KUNTI AND MADRI, TO A QUIET LIFE IN THE HIMALAYAS.

BUT ONE DAY —

DEAREST ONE, HOW I SORROW WHEN I SEE YOUR CHILDLESS STATE!

DO NOT GRIEVE, MY LORD. I KNOW OF A WAY OUT BUT I HAVE NOT TOLD YOU ABOUT IT.

WITH THE HELP OF THE MANTRA, KUNTI AND MADRI HAD FIVE SONS IN ALL — THE PANDAVA PRINCES.

WHEN PANDU DIED, MADRI BURNT HERSELF ON THE FUNERAL PYRE. KUNTI TOOK THE FIVE PRINCES, YUDHISHTHIRA (SON OF DHARMA), BHEEMA (SON OF VAYU), ARJUNA (SON OF INDRA), NAKULA AND SAHADEVA (SONS OF THE ASVINI TWINS), TO HASTINAPURA.

REVERED UNCLE BHEESHMA, AND WISE VIDURA, I LEAVE THE FATHERLESS SONS OF PANDU IN YOUR CARE.

THE PANDAVA PRINCES SHALL BE BROUGHT UP, AS THE HEIRS OF PANDU, ALONG WITH THEIR COUSINS THE KAURAVAS.

FROM THE BEGINNING A BITTER RIVALRY SPRANG UP BETWEEN THE COUSINS. THE KAURAVA PRINCES WERE UNHAPPY.

OUR COUSINS HAVE COME AND SPOILT OUR LIFE.

BHEEMA TORMENTS ME ON THE PLAYGROUND AND HAUNTS MY DREAMS.

AND KARNA WHO OFTEN CAME TO HASTINAPURA WATCHED.

BHEEMA IS UNFAIR! POOR DURYODHANA.

DRONACHARYA, MASTER IN THE PRINCELY ARTS, TAUGHT THE PRINCES.

ARJUNA'S SKILL IN ARCHERY IS UNMATCHED BY ANY OF US. I FEAR THOSE PRINCES WILL RULE US ONE DAY.

KARNA TOO BECAME HIS PUPIL. BUT—

HE IS PARTIAL TO ARJUNA. HE WILL NEVER LET ME SURPASS HIM.

GURU, PLEASE TEACH ME THE BRAHMASTRA.

THE BRAHMASTRA IS ONLY MEANT FOR BRAHMANAS, AND HIGH-BORN KSHATRIYAS. I CANNOT TEACH IT TO YOU— A CHARIOTEER'S SON.

KARNA WAS STUNG BY THESE WORDS.

PARASHURAMA, THEY SAY, HATES KSHATRIYAS. I WILL GO TO HIM IN THE GUISE OF A BRAHMAN. HE IS SURE TO ACCEPT ME AS HIS PUPIL.

WHEN HE REACHED THE ASHRAM OF THE GREAT SAGE —

I AM A BRAHMAN LAD. PLEASE ACCEPT ME AS YOUR PUPIL.

COME, MY SON. I AM WILLING TO TEACH ANY WORTHY YOUTH, WHO IS NOT A KSHATRIYA.

KARNA COULD NOT HELP THIS DECEPTION.

PARASHURAMA WAS VERY FOND OF HIS BRIGHT PUPIL.

YOU ARE NOW READY FOR THE MASTER WEAPON —THE BRAHMASTRA.

THEN ONE DAY WHILE PARASHURAMA WAS RESTING WITH HIS HEAD ON KARNA'S LAP –

AH! HOW THE LITTLE INSECT STINGS. BUT I WILL NOT DISTURB YOUR REST, BELOVED MASTER. SLEEP ON.

AND THE WOUND BLED BUT KARNA DID NOT STIR.

WHEN THE SAGE WOKE UP AND SAW THE BLOOD –

YOU HAVE DECEIVED ME. ONLY A KSHATRIYA CAN BEAR SUCH PAIN TO PROTECT ANOTHER. TELL ME THE TRUTH!

KARNA CONFESSED.

I AM THE SON OF ADHIRATHA, THE CHARIOTEER, A SUTAPUTRA. FORGIVE ME, SIR.

THE ENRAGED SAGE CURSED KARNA.

FOR DECEIVING YOUR GURU, YOUR KNOWLEDGE WILL FAIL YOU WHEN YOU NEED IT MOST!

AS HE WALKED AWAY, THE TOTALLY DEJECTED KARNA HARDLY KNEW WHERE HE WAS GOING.

SUDDENLY AN ANIMAL RUSHED PAST AND WITHOUT THINKING HE DREW HIS BOW AND KILLED IT.

AS HE WALKED TOWARDS THE DEAD ANIMAL —

A BRAHMAN WAVED ANGRILY AT HIM.

SINNER, YOU HAVE KILLED MY POOR INNOCENT COW.

IGNORING KARNA'S ATTEMPTS TO EXPLAIN, THE BRAHMAN CURSED HIM.

YOU TOO WILL BE KILLED WHEN YOU ARE HELPLESS TO DEFEND YOURSELF. EVEN AS YOU KILLED MY HELPLESS COW.

KARNA SADLY RETURNED TO THE ONE PERSON WHO KNEW AND LOVED HIM – HIS MOTHER.

IT SEEMS AS IF FATE IS AGAINST ME. I WONDER WHAT FURTHER HUMILIATIONS SHE HAS IN STORE FOR ME.

HE STAYED WITH HER A FEW DAYS. THEN ONE DAY –

MOTHER, I HEAR THAT AN OPEN TOURNAMENT IS TO BE HELD AT HASTINA- PURA. I WILL COMPETE. A VALIANT WARRIOR WILL FIND HIS PLACE AMONG THE VALIANT.

WHAT KARNA HAD HEARD WAS TRUE.

YOU ARE READY FOR AN EXHIBITION AND AN OPEN CONTEST OF YOUR SKILLS.

AFTER A CONSULTATION WITH THE KURU ELDERS, THE DAY WAS FIXED.

WITH HIS SPLENDID FEATS ARJUNA WAS EASILY THE CHAMPION OF THE DAY.

SUDDENLY THERE WAS A COMMOTION AND ALL EYES WERE TURNED TOWARDS THE ENTRANCE. A FIGURE ENTERED ON THE SCENE— IT WAS **KARNA**.

HE WAS ABLE TO PERFORM ALL ARJUNA'S FEATS.

DURYODHANA WAS JUBILANT.

WELCOME, O VALIANT ONE! IT IS OUR GOOD FORTUNE THAT YOU ARE HERE TODAY. WHAT SHALL BE YOUR REWARD?

KARNA WAS OVERWHELMED BY THIS WELCOME FROM DURYODHANA.

GOOD KING ALL I ASK IS YOUR LOVE AND THE OPPORTUNITY TO MEET DRONA'S FAVOURITE PUPIL ARJUNA IN SINGLE COMBAT!

IT SHALL BE DONE!

AS ARJUNA WAS GETTING READY, KRIPA, A TEACHER IN THE KURU PALACE, STEPPED FORWARD.

WHO ARE YOU? REVEAL YOUR PARENTAGE. OUR PRINCE MAY FIGHT ONLY WITH HIS EQUAL IN BIRTH AND STATUS.

MY GLORY WAS SHORT-LIVED. HOW SHALL I ANSWER HIM? O HEARTLESS MOTHER WHO ABANDONED ME AT BIRTH, WHO AM I?

14

THE NOBLE DURYODHANA CAME TO HIS RESCUE.

I CROWN KARNA PRINCE OF ANGA.

JUST THEN ADHIRATHA WALKED FEEBLY TOWARDS THE STAGE.

MY SON! MY BLESSINGS!

BHEEMA SUDDENLY ROARED WITH AMUSEMENT.

GO SUTAPUTRA! GO DRIVE YOUR CHARIOT! YOU ARE NOT WORTHY OF DEATH AT ARJUNA'S HANDS.

DURYODHANA COULD HARDLY CONTAIN HIS ANGER AS HE LED KARNA AWAY FROM THE HUMI--LIATING SCENE.

COME KARNA! IT TAKES A HERO TO RECOGNISE A HERO!

AS THEY DROVE AWAY IN DURYODHANA'S CHARIOT—

IT IS STRANGE! I FEEL SAFE FROM THE PANDAVAS, ALREADY. WHAT POWER DOES THIS KARNA HAVE THAT MAKES ME FEEL SO?

DURYODHANA YOU HAVE NOT BEFRIENDED ME IN VAIN. I WILL KILL ARJUNA IN SINGLE COMBAT ONE DAY! I WILL!

AS THE YEARS PASSED, RELATIONS BETWEEN THE COUSINS ONLY WORSENED. KARNA, IMPELLED BY HIS LOVE FOR DURYODHANA, BLINDLY TOOK HIS SIDE. YUDHISH-THIRA WAS CHEATED AT A GAME OF DICE, DEPRIVED OF HIS KING-DOM AND BANISHED FOR THIRTEEN YEARS, WITH HIS BROTHERS AND QUEEN DRAUPADI. AT THE END OF THE PERIOD THE PANDAVAS OPTED FOR A PEACEFUL SETTLE-MENT. BUT DURYODHANA, ENCOUR-AGED BY KARNA, AND AGAINST THE WISHES OF HIS ELDERS, REFUSED TO NEGOTIATE. IF THE PANDAVAS WANTED THEIR KINGDOM THEY WOULD HAVE TO FIGHT FOR IT.

IN THE HEAVENS INDRA WAS CONCERNED ABOUT ARJUNA...

IF KARNA IS DEPRIVED OF HIS KAVACHA AND KUNDALAS, MY SON ARJUNA NEED FEAR NO MORTAL.

...AND SURYA ABOUT KARNA.

IF INDRA INTERVENES, MY SON HAS NO CHANCE. I MUST WARN KARNA

SURYA TRIED TO WARN HIS SON IN A DREAM.

LORD INDRA WILL TRY TO TAKE ADVANTAGE OF YOUR GENEROSITY. DO NOT PART WITH YOUR KAVACHA AND KUNDALAS

INDRA APPROACHED KARNA IN THE GUISE OF A BRAHMAN.

I BEG FOR ALMS. KARNA, IT IS SAID, REFUSES NOTHING TO THOSE WHO ASK. I WANT YOUR KAVACHA AND KUNDALAS.

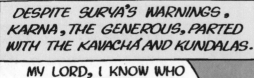

DESPITE SURYA'S WARNINGS, KARNA, THE GENEROUS, PARTED WITH THE KAVACHA AND KUNDALAS.

MY LORD, I KNOW WHO YOU ARE AND WHY YOU ARE HERE. YET, I GIVE TO YOU MY VERY LIFE. NEVER LET IT BE SAID THAT KARNA REFUSED ANYONE ANYTHING.

INDRA WAS TOUCHED.

IN RETURN I GRANT YOU MY MASTER WEAPON SHAKTI, BUT YOU MAY USE IT ONLY ONCE.

THE PANDAVAS MEANWHILE STILL HOPED FOR A PEACEFUL SETTLEMENT.

KRISHNA, IF WE CAN AVOID WAR, I'D BE HAPPY.

I WILL TRY TO CONVINCE THE KAURAVAS TO GIVE YOU YOUR SHARE.

KRISHNA WENT TO HASTINAPURA. BUT—

I HAVE FAILED! DURYODHANA IS BENT UPON WAR. HE DEPENDS ON KARNA TO WIN IT FOR HIM. IT IS TIME KARNA KNEW THE TRUTH ABOUT HIS BIRTH.

KRISHNA WENT TO KARNA AND TOLD HIM THE STORY OF HIS BIRTH. WHEN HE FINISHED —

COME WITH ME. I WILL MAKE YOU A GREAT EMPEROR. YOU WILL HAVE FIVE POWERFUL BROTHERS AND A MOTHER WHO LONGS FOR YOU.

KARNA WAS IN A TERRIBLE PREDICAMENT.

DURYODHANA'S LOVE IS WHAT I VALUE MOST IN MY LIFE. SO IF YOU REALLY HAVE MY INTEREST AT HEART PROMISE ME THAT YOU WILL KEEP THE SECRET OF MY BIRTH TILL I DIE.

I WILL!

WHEN KUNTI HEARD THAT KRISHNA'S TALKSHAD FAILED, SHE WAS FULL OF GRIEF.

I MUST NOW TELL KARNA WHO HE IS. THE WAR MAY YET BE AVERTED.

SHE WENT TO KARNA WHEN HE WAS AT THE END OF HIS MIDDAY PRAYERS.

MY MOTHER! HERE! WHAT CAN SHE WANT?

WHAT CAN I DO FOR YOU, O QUEEN?

SHE TOO RELATED TO KARNA THE STORY OF HIS BIRTH AND PLEADED WITH HIM NOT TO FIGHT HIS BROTHERS.

SEE, EVEN LORD SURYA, YOUR FATHER, JOINS ME IN MY REQUEST.

MOTHER, WHAT YOU ASK ME TO DO IS AGAINST MY DHARMA.

BUT HE WOULD NOT LET HIS MOTHER'S PLEAS GO IN VAIN.

I WILL FIGHT AGAINST YOUR SONS, MY BROTHERS, BUT I WILL NOT KILL ANY EXCEPT ARJUNA. YOU SHALL STILL HAVE FIVE SONS ALIVE AND I MY HONOUR.

KUNTI BLESSED KARNA AND LEFT HIM WITH MIXED FEELINGS.

BHEESHMA WAS TO LEAD THE KAURAVA ARMY. WHEN KARNA HEARD THAT, HE WENT TO DURYODHANA.

BHEESHMA HAS NEVER LIKED ME, AND I WILL NOT TAKE ORDERS FROM HIM. I WILL ENTER THE FIELD ONLY WHEN HE HAS FALLEN.

AND SO THE BATTLE OF KURUKSHETRA BECAME A REALITY. IT LASTED FOR 18 LONG DAYS. MANY VALIANT MEN WERE LOST ON EITHER SIDE. THE VENERABLE COMMANDER BHEESHMA, OF THE KAURAVA ARMIES, FELL ON THE TENTH DAY. HE FELL ON A BED OF ARROWS — STICKING OUT FROM HIS OWN ARMOUR. KARNA HAD ALWAYS LONGED FOR THE GRANDSIRE'S LOVE. WHEN HE HEARD THAT HE LAY WOUNDED, KARNA RUSHED TO THE SPOT.

MY LORD! I HAVE NEVER BEEN FORTUNATE ENOUGH TO BE LIKED BY YOU. YET I HAVE COME TO PAY MY RESPECTS TO YOU AND TO ASK FOR YOUR BLESSINGS.

DEAR KARNA! I KNEW WHO YOU WERE. YOUR FIRM LOYALTY TO DURYODHANA IS YOUR CHOSEN DHARMA. MAY YOU LEAD HIS FORCES TO VICTORY! GO FIGHT YOUR FATED ENEMIES.

IN A HURRIED COUNCIL, IT WAS DECIDED THAT DRONA SHOULD NOW COMMAND THE KAURAVA FORCES.

I DID HOPE THAT YOU WOULD LEAD US, KARNA.

IT IS BEST THAT DRONA LEAD US. LET THERE BE NO JEALOUSY AMONG OUR HEROES AT THIS STAGE.

AND SO THE BATTLE RAGED ON. IT WAS THE FOURTEENTH DAY. KARNA WAS ENGAGED IN FIGHTING BHEEMA. KARNA COULD EASILY HAVE KILLED HIM, BUT —

FORGIVE ME, DURYODHANA. I HAVE BHEEMA AT MY MERCY BUT I CANNOT KILL HIM. I HAVE PROMISED MY MOTHER. AH! ARJUNA COMES TO DEFEND BHEEMA. I AM LUCKY.

THAT DAY THE BATTLE CONTINUED INTO THE NIGHT. THIS WAS LUCKY FOR BHEEMA'S SON GHATOTKACHA AND HIS RAKSHASA FORCES, FOR RAKSHASAS ARE STRONGEST AT NIGHT.

KILL THAT FELLOW IMMEDIATELY, KARNA. OR ELSE OUR WHOLE ARMY WILL BE VANQUISHED.

THE ILL-FATED KARNA, IN THE HEAT OF BATTLE, FORGOT HIMSELF AND USED THE INFALLIBLE SHAKTI-THE WEAPON OF INDRA.

ONCE MORE THE GODS HAD SMILED ON THE FAVOURED ARJUNA.

ALAS! I HAVE KILLED GHATOTKACHA BUT I HAVE LOST THE MIGHTIEST WEAPON SHAKTI WHICH I HAD MEANT TO USE ON ARJUNA.

ON THE FIFTEENTH DAY OF THE BATTLE, DRONA WAS SLAIN AND THE KAURAVA HEROES SPOKE AS ONE IN FAVOUR OF KARNA AS THEIR NEXT COMMANDER.

THE INDESTRUCTIBLE KARNA SHALL BE THE COMMANDER OF OUR FORCES.

DURYODHANA WAS PLEASED.

KARNA, YOU HATE THE PANDAVAS AS MUCH AS I DO. I AM SURE OF OUR VICTORY NOW.

KARNA WAS GLAD THAT HE COULD AT LAST REPAY HIS BELOVED KING.

I WILL LEAD OUR FORCES TO VICTORY, MY KING! ARJUNA SHALL DIE AT MY HANDS.

AND THUS KARNA ASSUMED COMMAND OF THE KAURAVA FORCES. THAT DAY HE HAD NAKULA AT HIS MERCY.

MY CHILD, BE PROUD THAT YOU FOUGHT A DUEL WITH KARNA. NOW GO HOME TO ARJUNA AND TAKE CARE OF YOURSELF.

I WOULD RATHER HE KILLED ME. OH THE SHAME OF IT!

ONE MORE DAY HAS PASSED AND ARJUNA STILL LIVES.

IT SHALL BE DONE!

IT IS THE SKILL OF KRISHNA, HIS CHARIOTEER, THAT KEEPS HIM ALIVE. IF ONLY YOU COULD CONVINCE SHALYA TO BE MY CHARIOTEER, VICTORY WILL BE OURS.

KARNA LEFT DURYODHANA AND WENT TO HIS TENT. THERE, AS HE LAY AWAKE—

TOMORROW I FIGHT ARJUNA AND I MUST HONESTLY TRY TO KILL HIM. BUT I KNOW MY CHANCES ARE POOR.

HE TOSSED ABOUT RESTLESSLY. IT WAS A DIFFICULT NIGHT FOR HIM.

TOMORROW I WILL TRY TO FIGHT AND SPARE YUDHISHTHIRA TOO. MOTHER KUNTI MUST KNOW HOW I KEPT MY PROMISE.

HOW I LONGED FOR HER LOVE AND RECOGNITION! AND IN THESE MOMENTS, HOW I TREASURE THE BOUNDLESS LOVE OF MOTHER RADHA AND MY NOBLE DURYODHANA.

THIS LAST THOUGHT FINALLY LULLED HIM TO SLEEP.

THE NEXT DAY KARNA HAD HIS WISH TO ENGAGE YUDHISHTHIRA IN SINGLE COMBAT.

ARJUNA SHALL AVENGE ME.

I SPARE YOUR LIFE, YUDHISHTHIRA. YOU CAN NEVER KILL ME IN SINGLE COMBAT. LEAVE YOUR SUPERIORS TO THEIR EQUALS.

WHEN ARJUNA HEARD OF YUDHISHTHIRA'S HUMILIATION, HE COULD NOT WAIT TO ATTACK KARNA. HE SOON HAD THE CHANCE.

HOW WELL MY BROTHER WIELDS HIS WEAPONS!

HE FIGHTS LIKE A KING. IT IS HARD TO BELIEVE THAT HE IS ONLY A CHARIOTEER'S SON!

ALAS! FOR KARNA THE END WAS DRAWING NEAR. A WHEEL OF HIS CHARIOT SANK INTO THE GROUND.

MY MEMORY FAILS ME. I CANNOT RECALL THE MANTRAS OF THE GREAT PARASHURAMA!

WHILE HE JUMPED DOWN AND TRIED TO DRAG IT OUT, ARJUNA WAS AT AN ADVANTAGE. PARASHURAMA'S CURSE HAD TAKEN EFFECT.

WHEN KARNA WAS THUS HELPLESS, ARJUNA, WITH KRISHNA'S PROMPTING ....

.... SHOT AN ARROW THAT SEVERED THE HEAD OF THE GREAT HERO FROM ITS BEAUTIFUL BODY.

TWANG

THE CURSE OF THE BRAHMAN HAD NOT BEEN IN VAIN.

WHEN KUNTI HEARD OF KARNA'S DEATH —

DEAR, DEAR, SON! I CAST YOU OFF AT BIRTH AND YOUR DEATH I CAN BUT LAMENT IN PRIVATE.

AFTER THE BATTLE, THE VICTORIOUS PANDAVAS PERFORMED THE DEATH CEREMONIES FOR THE DEAD.

WILL I HAVE THE COURAGE TO SEND YOUR SOUL ON ITS JOURNEY AS BEFITS YOUR BIRTH?

JUST AS YUDHISHTHIRA HAD ENDED WITH THE LAST OFFERING TO THEIR KINSMEN —

WAIT! THERE IS ONE MORE LEFT.

WHO IS IT THAT I HAVE FORGOTTEN?

KARNA!

BUT WHY SHOULD I DO IT FOR KARNA? KARNA, OUR ARCH ENEMY, KARNA THE CHARIOTEER'S SON!

31

KUNTI THEN BROKE DOWN AND TOLD HER TALE.

THE SUN SMILED. EACH OF THE PANDAVAS REMEMBERED HIS OWN ENCOUNTER WITH THE DEAD BROTHER AND THIER HEARTS REACHED OUT TO HIM.

THUS KARNA WHO HAD LONGED FOR LOVE, RECOGNITION AND A GOOD NAME, WHILE HE LIVED, SECURED THESE, LIKE MANY GREAT MEN AFTER HIM, ONLY BY HIS DEATH.

ABHIMANYU

STAR-CROSSED PRINCE

The route to your roots

ABHIMANYU

The Kauravas had made a fateful error. Lusting after their cousins' kingdom, they underestimated young Abhimanyu's determination and ability to defend it. Brilliantly distilled in this handsome and much-loved Pandava prince were his father Arjuna's courage, Lord Krishna's wisdom, and the patience, strength and gentle humility of his uncles. Even as he thwarted his enemies' ambitions, Abhimanyu earned their grudging admiration and a very special place in the saga of the Mahabharata.

Script
Kamala Chandrakant

Illustrations
Pratap Mulick

Editor
Anant Pai

ABHIMANYU

ABHIMANYU, THE SON OF ARJUNA, THE PANDAVA AND SUBHADRA, KRISHNA'S SISTER, IS RENOWNED FOR THE VALOUR DISPLAYED BY HIM IN THE MAHABHARATA WAR.

HIS FATHER, ARJUNA COULD NOT HELP LOVING HIM MORE THAN HIS OTHER SONS.

ABHIMANYU SHALL GROW UP TO BE THE FOREMOST AMONG THE PANDAVAS AS WELL AS THE YADAVAS!

HUSH! ONE OUGHT NOT TO PRAISE ONE'S OWN CHILD THUS.

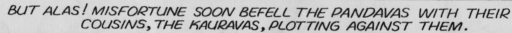

BUT ALAS! MISFORTUNE SOON BEFELL THE PANDAVAS WITH THEIR COUSINS, THE KAURAVAS, PLOTTING AGAINST THEM.

THE PANDAVAS ARE BECOMING TOO POWERFUL.

WE MUST TAKE THEIR KINGDOM AND GET RID OF THEM SOMEHOW!

I HAVE IT! YUDHISHTHIRA HAS A WEAKNESS FOR GAMBLING. LET US INVITE HIM TO A GAME AND MAKE THE DICE OBEY US.

THE KAURAVAS CARRIED OUT THEIR WICKED PLOT.

YUDHISHTHIRA, YOU'VE LOST AGAIN.

YOU HAD PLEDGED YOUR KINGDOM. NOW GIVE IT UP. GO INTO EXILE WITH YOUR BROTHERS INTO THE FORESTS FOR THIRTEEN YEARS.

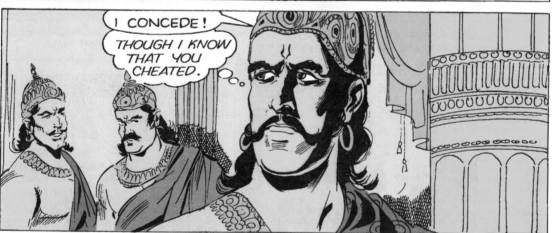

I CONCEDE!

THOUGH I KNOW THAT YOU CHEATED.

THE PANDAVAS SET OUT FOR THE FORESTS WITH THE SORROWFUL CITIZENS WHO HAD GATHERED TO BID THEM FAREWELL, IN ATTENDANCE.

ABHIMANYU WAS A MERE CHILD WHEN THESE EVENTS TOOK PLACE. BUT HE WAS WELL LOOKED AFTER BY HIS MOTHER.

YOUR VALOUR SHALL ONE DAY AVENGE THIS HUMILIATION.

HE GREW UP TO BE A VALIANT YOUTH AND KRISHNA'S FAVOURITE NEPHEW.

I SHALL FIGHT THE KAURAVAS AND WIN BACK OUR KINGDOM.

WELL SPOKEN, ABHIMANYU, WELL SPOKEN!

HE WAS LOVED AND ADMIRED BY ALL WHO KNEW HIM.

ABHIMANYU HAS INHERITED THE QUALITIES OF KRISHNA AND THE PANDAVAS.

YES. HE HAS YUDHISHTHIRA'S PATIENCE, KRISHNA'S CONDUCT, BHIMA'S STRENGTH, THE GENTLENESS OF NAKULA AND SAHADEVA AND ARJUNA'S LOOKS, PROWESS AND SCRIPTURAL KNOWLEDGE.

MEANWHILE THIRTEEN YEARS HAD PASSED. THE PANDAVAS WERE AT THE COURT OF KING VIRATA, IN DISGUISE AND IN THE LAST YEAR OF THEIR EXILE.

WHILE THERE, ARJUNA HELPED VIRATA'S SON UTTARA TO TRIUMPH OVER A KAURAVA ATTACK.

AFTER ARJUNA AND UTTARA RETURNED FROM THE BATTLE, THE PANDAVAS DISCLOSED THEIR IDENTITY TO VIRATA.

BHIMA.

I AM ARJUNA.

I AM YUDHISHTHIRA.

NAKULA.

SAHADEVA.

ARJUNA, I OFFER YOU MY DAUGHTER UTTARĀ.

O KING, I ACCEPT YOUR DAUGHTER AS MY DAUGHTER-IN-LAW.

WHY NOT AS YOUR WIFE?

I CANNOT. I WAS HER TEACHER ONCE IN MUSIC AND DANCE.

MY SON, THE VALIANT AND GODLIKE ABHIMANYU, IS KRISHNA'S FAVOURITE NEPHEW. HE SURPASSES ALL IN LOOKS AND IN THE KNOWLEDGE OF WEAPONS. HE IS FIT TO BE YOUR SON-IN-LAW AND UTTARA'S HUSBAND.

VIRATA WAS AGREEABLE.

WITH YOU AS THE FATHER OF MY SON-IN-LAW, I HAVE NOTHING ELSE TO ASK FOR.

YUDHISHTHIRA, TOO, GAVE HIS ASSENT AND WORD WAS SENT TO KRISHNA TO BRING SUBHADRA AND ABHIMANYU AND THEIR KINSMEN TO VIRATA'S KINGDOM.

THE WEDDING OF ABHIMANYU AND UTTARA WAS SOLEMNISED AMIDST GREAT FEASTING AND REJOICING. IT WAS ATTENDED BY A HOST OF FRIENDLY KINGS OF NEIGHBOURING KINGDOMS.

AFTER THE WEDDING THE PANDAVAS HELD A COUNCIL.

I WOULD LIKE TO WIN BACK OUR KINGDOM WITHOUT BLOODSHED.

LET ME GO TO HASTINAPURA AND SEE WHAT I CAN DO.

BUT KING DURYODHANA, THE KAURAVA, WAS OBSTINATE.

I REFUSE THEM EVEN AN INCH OF LAND. LET THEM FIGHT AND TAKE IT IF THEY CAN.

KRISHNA'S MISS ON FAILED.

AND IT WAS WAR BETWEEN THE PANDAVAS AND THE KAURAVAS – THE TERRIBLE WAR OF THE MAHABHARATA – IN WHICH PRACTICALLY ALL THE KINGS OF THOSE TIMES FOUGHT, AS ALLIES, ON ONE SIDE OR THE OTHER.

IT IS NOT YET NOON AND OUR ARMY IS BEING ROUTED BY THE KAURAVAS.

BHEESHMA, THE GRANDSIRE IS CREATING HAVOC WHEREVER HE GOES.

ABHIMANYU WHEN HE HEARD THIS CHARGED UPON BHEESHMA.

A MERE STRIPLING OF A BOY BUT WHAT A FINE WARRIOR! HE SEEMS TO BE EVERYWHERE.

THUS ABHIMANYU DISTINGUISHED HIMSELF ON THE VERY FIRST DAY OF THE BATTLE.

SOON OTHER WARRIORS CAME TO RELIEVE HIM AND BHEESHMA TURNED HIS ATTENTION TO THEM. BUT THE FIRST DAY WAS A BAD ONE FOR THE PANDAVAS. THAT NIGHT—

BHEESHMA HAS DECIMATED OUR ARMIES ON THIS VERY FIRST DAY OF BATTLE.

WHY DO YOU WORRY? YOU HAVE VALIANT BROTHERS, NEPHEWS AND ALLIES. MOREOVER SHIKHANDI IS DESTINED TO BE THE CAUSE OF BHEESHMA'S DEATH.

THUS KRISHNA CONSOLED AND ENCOURAGED THE PANDAVAS.

ON THE SECOND DAY, THE KAURAVAS INTOXICATED BY THEIR EARLY VICTORY, WERE OVER CONFIDENT AND CARELESS. TILL—

IT IS WISE TO END THE FIGHT FOR THE DAY AND RETIRE. WE HAVE SUFFERED HEAVY REVERSES AND OUR TROOPS ARE WEARY.

AND THE PANDAVAS WON THE DAY.

SO THE BATTLE WENT ON, SOMETIMES FAVOURING THE PANDAVAS, SOMETIMES THE KAURAVAS.

TILL AT LAST ON THE TENTH DAY BHEESHMA FELL, AT THE HANDS OF ARJUNA SHIELDED BY SHIKHANDI.

DRONA WAS MADE COMMANDER OF THE KAURAVA ARMIES.

WITH YOU AS OUR LEADER WE CAN EASILY DEFEAT YUDHISHTHIRA AND HIS MIGHTY ALLIES.

AND THE GREATEST BOON YOU COULD GIVE ME WOULD BE TO CAPTURE YUDHISHTHIRA ALIVE!

DRONA TRIED BUT FAILED. THAT EVENING THE KAURAVAS HELD A SPECIAL CONFERENCE.

WE CAN NEVER TAKE YUDHISHTHIRA AS LONG AS ARJUNA IS BY HIS SIDE.

THE PLOY WAS SUCCESSFUL. ARJUNA WAS DRAWN AWAY, AND DRONA ATTACKED. THE ATTACK WAS SO FIERCE THAT THE PANDAVAS WITH ARJUNA AWAY, WERE LOSING GROUND.

AT LAST YUDHISHTHIRA APPROACHED ABHIMANYU, PLACING THE BURDEN ON HIS YOUNG SHOULDERS.

ONLY YOU, ARJUNA, KRISHNA AND PRADYUMNA KNOW HOW TO BREAK THROUGH DRONA'S CIRCULAR FORMATION OF TROOPS. NONE OF THEM IS HERE, BUT YOU.

SON, WILL YOU LEAD US?

I WILL GLADLY TRY TO BREAK THROUGH THE FORMATION BUT......

...I DO NOT KNOW HOW TO COME OUT OF IT, IF I AM OVERPOWERED AND IN DANGER.

BREAK THE FORMATION AND MAKE WAY FOR US TO ENTER. WE WILL FOLLOW CLOSE UPON YOUR HEELS AND PROTECT YOU.

I WILL BREAK THROUGH IT AND SLAUGHTER THE KAURAVAS. MY ACHIEVEMENT TODAY SHALL EMBELLISH THE FAIR NAME OF THE PANDAVAS AND THE YADAVAS.

MAY YOUR MIGHT INCREASE EVEN AS YOU SPEAK.

ABHIMANYU COMMANDED HIS CHARIOTEER.

PROCEED! PROCEED! URGE THE HORSES TOWARDS DRONA'S TROOPS.

THE PANDAVAS HAVE PLACED A HEAVY BURDEN ON YOU TODAY. THINK WELL BEFORE YOU PROCEED.

DRONA IS AN ADEPT IN THE ART OF WARFARE. YOU HAVE BEEN BROUGHT UP IN COMFORT AND ARE NOT USED TO THE STRAIN OF WAR.

I AM ARJUNA'S SON AND KRISHNA'S NEPHEW. DRIVE ON.

THEY REACHED DRONA'S ARRAY WITH THE PANDAVAS AND THEIR ALLIES FOLLOWING CLOSE BEHIND.

LOOK! HERE HE COMES! ABHIMANYU!

THEN LIKE A PROUD YOUNG LION FALLING UPON A HERD OF ELEPHANTS, ABHIMANYU RUSHED AT DRONA.

THE HEROES FOUGHT ON AND THE TROOPS SLAUGHTERED ONE ANOTHER.

WHILE THE TERRIFYING BATTLE RAGED, ABHIMANYU, BREAKING THE CIRCULAR ARRAY, ENTERED IT UNDER THE VERY NOSE OF DRONA.

HE IS INDEED THE GREATEST AMONG ARCHERS! HE IS CAPABLE OF DESTROYING AN ENTIRE ARMY IF HE CHOOSES!

BUT ALAS FOR HIM, BEFORE THE PANDAVAS AND THEIR WARRIORS COULD FOLLOW HIM, THE BREACH WAS EFFICIENTLY AND EFFECTIVELY CLOSED BY JAYADRATHA.

AND ABHIMANYU WAS ALONE.

BUT HE FOUGHT BRAVELY AND FELLED THE KAURAVA WARRIORS, COVERING THE EARTH WITH THEIR MUTILATED BODIES.

THE KAURAVA TROOPS TERRIFIED BY THIS ONSLAUGHT, TRIED TO FLEE ON CHARIOTS AND ELEPHANTS FORSAKING THEIR WOUNDED KINSMEN AND FRIENDS.

WHEN DURYODHANA SAW HIS ARMY BEING THUS ROUTED BY ABHIMAN-YU, HE WAS FURIOUS AND RUSHED TOWARDS HIM.

DRONA WAS ALARMED.

SAVE THE KING! ABHIMANYU KILLS ALL MEN HE AIMS AT. AND NOW HIS AIM IS ON THE KING OF THE KAURAVAS.

A GREAT NUMBER OF WARRIORS IMMEDIATELY WENT TO DURYODHANA'S RESCUE.

AND SUCCEEDED IN DRAWING HIM AWAY.

BUT ABHIMANYU WAS ENRAGED WHEN HE FOUND HIS PRIZE TARGET BEING SNATCHED AWAY.

HE VENTED HIS ANGER ON THE WARRIORS WHO HAD PROTECTED DURYODHANA.

FORGETTING THE CODE OF WAR CONDUCT, A NUMBER OF WARRIORS, LED BY DRONA, JOINTLY ATTACKED YOUNG ABHIMANYU.

NOW HE CAN'T ESCAPE DEATH AT OUR HANDS.

IT SEEMED IMPOSSIBLE TO CONTROL THEIR ADVANCES. BUT A SHOWER OF ARROWS FROM ABHIMANYU'S BOW HELD THEM.

ONE OF THE WARRIORS, ASMAKA, RUSHED HIS CHARIOT AT GREAT SPEED TOWARDS ABHIMANYU.

ABHIMANYU'S ARROW KILLED HIM.

KARNA THEN MADE A DASH TOWARDS ABHIMANYU.

BUT HIS ARMOUR WAS PIERCED.

ABHIMANYU THEN WOUNDED SHALYA SO BADLY THAT THE GREAT WARRIOR COULD NOT EVEN MOVE FROM HIS SEAT.

SHALYA'S BROTHER RUSHED FORWARD.

I MUST AVENGE THE DEFEAT OF MY BROTHER.

ONE SINGLE ARROW FROM ABHIMANYU'S BOW...

...BROKE HIS CHARIOT TO PIECES.

SO GREAT WAS THE SKILL DISPLAYED BY ABHIMANYU THAT EVEN DRONA WHO LED THE ATTACK, ADMIRED HIM.

HE STANDS UNEQUALLED AS A BOWMAN. IF HE WISHES HE CAN WIPE OUT THIS WHOLE HOST, SINGLE-HANDED.

DURYODHANA, WHO OVERHEARD THIS REMARK, BECAME VERY ANGRY.

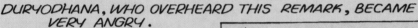

DUHSHASANA! LISTEN! HOW PARTIAL DRONACHARYA IS TOWARDS ARJUNA'S SON. WE MUST KILL THE BOY SOON.

I'LL KILL HIM. THIS VERY INSTANT.

THE CHARIOTS OF ABHIMANYU AND DUHSHASANA MADE WONDERFUL MOVEMENTS AGAINST EACH OTHER.

VERY SOON, DUHSHASANA FELL SENSELESS IN HIS CHARIOT, STRUCK BY ONE OF ABHIMANYU'S ARROWS.

DUHSHASANA'S CHARIOTEER RUSHED AWAY FROM THE BATTLE SCENE TO SAVE HIS MASTER.

IT WAS NOW KARNA'S TURN. HE SENT A SHOWER OF ARROWS.

ABHIMANYU INTERCEPTED THEM ALL.

AND SENT A FRESH SHOWER OF ARROWS IN THE DIRECTION OF KARNA.

KARNA HAD TO RETREAT.

DURYODHANA'S SON, LAKSHMANA, A BRAVE WARRIOR, RUSHED TOWARDS ABHIMANYU IN A BID TO SAVE THE HONOUR OF THE KAURAVA ARMY.

KARNA, DRONA AND MANY OTHER RETREATING WARRIORS, NOW CAME BACK TO SUPPORT LAKSHMANA IN HIS FIGHT.

BUT A SHARP ARROW FROM ABHIMAN-YU'S BOW CAME WHIZZING...

...AND PIERCED LAKSHMANA.

SEEING THE DEAD BODY OF HIS YOUNG SON, DURYODHANA WAS FURIOUS.

KILL! KILL THE WICKED ABHIMANYU!

AT THIS COMMAND OF DURYODHANA, DRONA, KARNA AND THE OTHER WARRIORS IN THE KAURAVA ARMY MOUNTED A FRESH ATTACK ON ABHIMANYU.

KARNA TURNED TO DRONA.

TELL US HOW TO KILL HIM BEFORE HE SLAYS US ALL.

YOU WILL NEVER BE ABLE TO PIERCE HIS ARMOUR.

AIM AT THE REINS OF HIS HORSES AND CUT THEM OFF. HE WILL BE DISABLED. THEN ATTACK FROM BEHIND.

KARNA CUT OFF THE REINS OF HIS HORSES.

FROM BEHIND, HE SHOT AN ARROW THAT BROKE ABHIMANYU'S BOW.

SOON ABHIMANYU'S HORSES LAY DEAD AND HIS CHARIOTEER WAS KILLED.

NOW HE JUMPED TO THE GROUND AND...

...WHIRLED HIS SWORD AND SHIELD. ALONE IN THE FIELD, HE HELD HIS GROUND AGAINST MANY WARRIORS.

SOON AN ARROW FROM DRONA BROKE HIS SWORD...

...AND AN ARROW FROM KARNA HIS SHIELD.

THUS ABHIMANYU WAS TOTALLY DISABLED. BUT UNDAUNTED, HE PICKED UP THE WHEEL OF HIS CHARIOT...

...AND BEGAN WHIRLING IT AGAINST HIS UNFAIR AND UNJUST ENEMIES. BUT HE WAS COMPLETELY ENCIRCLED.

ARROWS FROM MANY BOWS CAME WHIZZING FROM ALL DIRECTIONS.

AND SOON THE WHEEL LAY BROKEN TO PIECES.

ABHIMANYU THEN PICKED UP A MACE THAT WAS LYING ON THE FIELD.

DUHSHASANA'S SON CLOSED IN.

WHILE FIGHTING BOTH FELL TO THE GROUND.

BUT DUHSHASANA'S SON WAS THE FIRST TO GET UP.

AND BEFORE ABHIMANYU COULD RISE, HE BROUGHT THE MACE DOWN ON HIS SKULL.

WHEN THE MIGHTY HERO FELL, LIKE SAVAGES THE KAURAVA WARRIORS DANCED AROUND HIS DEAD BODY.

NOT ONE OF THEM, HOWEVER, OUTLIVED THE WAR. ARJUNA, BHEEMA AND THE MIGHTY PANDAVAS AVENGED ABHIMANYU BY KILLING THEM ALL IN THE BATTLES THAT FOLLOWED AT KURUKSHETRA ...

...AND ABHIMANYU'S BRAVERY IS REMEMBERED TILL THIS DAY.